LIVES OF THE POETS

E. L. DOCTOROW

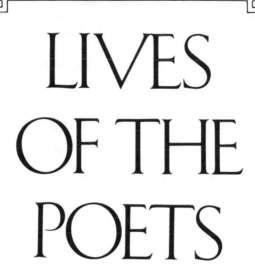

LIVES OF THE POETS

SIX STORIES AND A NOVELLA

RANDOM HOUSE
NEW YORK

Copyright © 1984 by E. L. Doctorow
All rights reserved under International and Pan-American
Copyright Conventions. Published in the United States by
Random House, Inc., New York, and simultaneously in Can-
ada by Random House of Canada Limited, Toronto.

Portions of this work have previously appeared in the following publications: *The Atlantic, Esquire, Vanity Fair,* and
The Paris Review.

Library of Congress Cataloging in Publication Data
Doctorow, E. L., 1931–
Lives of the poets.
Contents: The writer in the family—
The water works—Willi—[etc.]
I. Title.
PS3554.03L5   1984   813'.54   84–42513
ISBN 0-394-52530-2

Manufactured in the United States of America
Typography and binding design by J. K. Lambert
2 4 6 8 9 7 5 3
First Edition

To my brother

DON

CONTENTS

THE
WRITER
IN THE
FAMILY

▫   ▫   ▫

I N 1955 MY FATHER died with his ancient mother still alive in a nursing home. The old lady was ninety and hadn't even known he was ill. Thinking the shock might kill her, my aunts told her that he had moved to Arizona for his bronchitis. To the immigrant generation of my grandmother, Arizona was the American equivalent of the Alps, it was where you went for your health. More accurately, it was where you went if you had the money. Since my father had failed in all the business enterprises of his life, this was the aspect of the news my grandmother dwelled on, that he had finally had some success. And so it came about that as we mourned him at home in our stocking feet, my grandmother was bragging to her cronies about her son's new life in the dry air of the desert.

My aunts had decided on their course of action without consulting us. It meant neither my mother nor my brother nor I could visit Grandma because we were supposed to have moved west too, a family, after all. My brother Harold and I didn't mind—it was always a nightmare at the old people's home, where they all sat around staring at us while we tried to make conversation with Grandma. She looked terrible, had numbers of ailments, and her mind wandered. Not seeing her was no disappointment either for my mother, who had never gotten along with the old woman and did not visit when she could have. But what was disturbing was that my aunts had acted in the manner of that side of the family of making government on everyone's behalf, the true citizens by blood and the lesser citizens by marriage. It was exactly this attitude that had tormented my mother all her married life. She claimed Jack's family had never accepted her. She had battled them for twenty-five years as an outsider.

A few weeks after the end of our ritual mourning my Aunt Frances phoned us from her home in Larchmont. Aunt Frances was the wealthier of my father's sisters. Her husband was a lawyer, and both her sons were at Amherst. She had called to say that Grandma was asking why she didn't hear from Jack. I had answered the phone. "You're the writer in the family," my aunt said. "Your father had so much faith in you. Would you mind making up something? Send it to me and I'll read it to her. She won't know the difference."

That evening, at the kitchen table, I pushed my homework aside and composed a letter. I tried to imagine my father's response to his new life. He had never been west. He had never traveled anywhere. In his generation the great journey was from the working class to the professional class. He hadn't managed that either. But he loved New York, where he had been born and lived his life, and he was always discovering new things about it. He especially loved the old parts of the city below Canal Street, where he would find ships' chandlers or firms that wholesaled in spices and teas. He was a salesman for an appliance jobber with accounts all over the city. He liked to bring home rare cheeses or exotic foreign vegetables that were sold only in certain neighborhoods. Once he brought home a barometer, another time an antique ship's telescope in a wooden case with a brass snap.

"Dear Mama," I wrote. "Arizona is beautiful. The sun shines all day and the air is warm and I feel better than I have in years. The desert is not as barren as you would expect, but filled with wildflowers and cactus plants and peculiar crooked trees that look like men holding their arms out. You can see great distances in whatever direction you turn and to the west is a range of mountains maybe fifty miles from here, but in the morning with the sun on them you can see the snow on their crests."

My aunt called some days later and told me it was when she read this letter aloud to the old lady that the full effect of Jack's death came over her. She had to excuse herself and went out in the parking lot to cry. "I wept so," she said. "I felt such terrible longing for him. You're so right, he loved to go places, he loved life, he loved everything."

WE BEGAN trying to organize our lives. My father had borrowed money against his insurance and there was very little left. Some commissions were still due but it didn't look as if his firm would honor them. There was a couple of thousand dollars in a savings bank that had to be maintained there until the estate was settled. The lawyer involved was Aunt Frances' husband and he was very proper. "The estate!" my mother muttered, gesturing as if to pull out her hair. "The estate!" She applied for a job part-time in the admissions office of the hospital where my father's terminal illness had been diagnosed, and where he had spent some months until they had sent him home to die. She knew a lot of the doctors and staff and she had learned "from bitter experience," as she told them, about the hospital routine. She was hired.

I hated that hospital, it was dark and grim and full of tortured people. I thought it was masochistic of my mother to seek out a job there, but did not tell her so.

We lived in an apartment on the corner of 175th Street and the Grand Concourse, one flight up. Three rooms. I shared the bedroom with my brother. It was jammed with furniture because when my father had required a hospital bed in the last weeks of his illness we had moved some of the living-room pieces into the bedroom and made over the living room for him. We had to navigate bookcases, beds, a gateleg table, bureaus, a record player and radio console, stacks of 78 albums, my brother's trombone and music stand, and so on. My mother continued to sleep on the convertible sofa in the living room that had been their bed before his illness. The two rooms were connected by a narrow hall made even narrower by bookcases along the wall. Off the hall were a small kitchen and dinette and a bathroom. There were lots of appliances in the kitchen—broiler, toaster, pressure cooker, counter-top dishwasher, blender—that my father had gotten through his job, at cost. A treasured phrase in our house: *at cost.* But most of these fixtures went unused because my mother did not care for them. Chromium devices with timers or gauges that required the reading of elaborate instructions were not for her. They were in part responsible for the awful clutter of our lives and now she wanted to get rid of them. "We're being buried," she said. "Who needs them!"

So we agreed to throw out or sell anything inessential. While I found boxes for the appliances and my brother tied the boxes with twine, my mother opened my father's closet and took out his clothes. He had several suits because as a salesman he needed to look his best. My mother wanted us to try on his suits to see which of them could be altered and used. My brother refused to try them on. I tried on one jacket which was too large for me. The lining inside the sleeves chilled my arms and the vaguest scent of my father's being came to me.

"This is way too big," I said.

"Don't worry," my mother said. "I had it cleaned. Would I let you wear it if I hadn't?"

It was the evening, the end of winter, and snow was coming down on the windowsill and melting as it settled. The ceiling bulb glared on a pile of my father's suits and trousers on hangers flung across the bed in the shape of a dead man. We refused to try on anything more, and my mother began to cry.

"What are you crying for?" my brother shouted. "You wanted to get rid of things, didn't you?"

A FEW WEEKS later my aunt phoned again and said she thought it would be necessary to have another letter from Jack. Grandma had fallen out of her chair and bruised herself and was very depressed.

"How long does this go on?" my mother said.

"It's not so terrible," my aunt said, "for the little time left to make things easier for her."

My mother slammed down the phone. "He can't even die when he wants to!" she cried. "Even death comes second to Mama! What are they afraid of, the shock will kill her? Nothing can kill her. She's indestructible! A stake through the heart couldn't kill her!"

When I sat down in the kitchen to write the letter I found it more difficult than the first one. "Don't watch me," I said to my brother. "It's hard enough."

"You don't have to do something just because someone wants you to," Harold said. He was two years older than me and had started at City College; but when my father became ill he had switched to night school and gotten a job in a record store.

"Dear Mama," I wrote. "I hope you're feeling well. We're all fit as a fiddle. The life here is good and the people are very friendly and informal. Nobody wears suits and ties here. Just a pair of slacks and a short-sleeved shirt. Perhaps a sweater in the evening. I have bought into a very successful radio and record business and I'm doing very well. You remember Jack's Electric, my old place on Forty-third Street? Well, now it's Jack's Arizona Electric and we have a line of television sets as well."

I sent that letter off to my Aunt Frances, and as we all knew she would, she phoned soon after. My brother held his hand over the mouthpiece. "It's Frances with her latest review," he said.

"Jonathan? You're a very talented young man. I just wanted to tell you what a blessing your letter was. Her whole face lit up when I read the part about Jack's store. That would be an excellent way to continue."

"Well, I hope I don't have to do this anymore, Aunt Frances. It's not very honest."

Her tone changed. "Is your mother there? Let me talk to her."

"She's not here," I said.

"Tell her not to worry," my aunt said. "A poor old lady who has never wished anything but the best for her will soon die."

I did not repeat this to my mother, for whom it would have been one more in the family anthology of unforgivable remarks. But then I had to suffer it myself for the possible truth it might embody. Each side defended its position with rhetoric, but I, who wanted peace, rationalized the snubs and rebuffs each inflicted on the other, taking no stands, like my father himself.

Years ago his life had fallen into a pattern of business failures and missed opportunities. The great debate between his family on the one side, and my mother Ruth on the other, was this: who was responsible for the fact that he had not lived up to anyone's expectations?

As to the prophecies, when spring came my mother's prevailed. Grandma was still alive.

One balmy Sunday my mother and brother and I took the bus to the Beth El cemetery in New Jersey to visit my father's grave. It was situated on a slight rise. We stood looking over rolling fields embedded with monuments. Here and there processions of black cars wound their way through the lanes, or clusters of people stood at open graves. My father's grave was planted with tiny shoots of ever-green but it lacked a headstone. We had chosen one and paid for it and then the stonecutters had gone on strike. Without a headstone my father did not seem to be honorably dead. He didn't seem to me properly buried.

My mother gazed at the plot beside his, reserved for her coffin. "They were always too fine for other people," she said. "Even in the old days on Stanton Street. They put on airs. Nobody was ever good enough for them. Finally Jack himself was not good enough for them. Except to get them things wholesale. Then he was good enough for them."

"Mom, please," my brother said.

"If I had known. Before I ever met him he was tied to his mama's apron strings. And Essie's apron strings were like chains, let me tell you. We had to live where we could be near them for the Sunday visits. Every Sunday, that was my life, a visit to mamaleh. Whatever she knew I wanted, a better apartment, a stick of furniture, a sum-mer camp for the boys, she spoke against it. You know your father, every decision had to be considered and reconsidered. And nothing changed. Nothing ever changed."

She began to cry. We sat her down on a nearby bench. My brother walked off and read the names on stones. I looked at my mother, who was crying, and I went off after my brother.

"Mom's still crying," I said. "Shouldn't we do something?"

"It's all right," he said. "It's what she came here for."

"Yes," I said, and then a sob escaped from my throat. "But I feel like crying too."

My brother Harold put his arm around me. "Look at this old black stone here," he said. "The way it's carved. You can see the changing fashion in monuments—just like everything else."

S O M E W H E R E   in this time I began dreaming of my father. Not the robust father of my childhood, the handsome man with healthy pink skin and brown eyes and a mustache and the thinning hair parted in the middle. My dead father. We were taking him home from the hospital. It was understood that he had come back from death. This was amazing and joyous. On the other hand, he was terribly mysteriously damaged, or, more accurately, spoiled and unclean. He was very yellowed and debilitated by his death, and there were no guarantees that he wouldn't soon die again. He seemed aware of this and his entire personality was changed. He was angry and impatient with all of us. We were trying to help him in some way, struggling to get him home, but something prevented us, something we had to fix, a tattered suitcase that had sprung open, some mechanical thing: he had a car but it wouldn't start; or the car was made of wood; or his clothes, which had become too large for him, had caught in the door. In one version he was all bandaged and as we tried to lift him from his wheelchair into a taxi the bandage began to unroll and catch in the spokes of the wheelchair. This seemed to be some unreasonableness on his part. My mother looked on sadly and tried to get him to cooperate.

That was the dream. I shared it with no one. Once when I woke, crying out, my brother turned on the light. He wanted to know what I'd been dreaming but I pretended I didn't remember. The dream made me feel guilty. I felt guilty *in* the dream too because my enraged father knew we didn't want to live with him. The dream represented us taking him home, or trying to, but it was nevertheless understood by all of us that he was to live alone. He was this derelict back from death, but what we were doing was taking him to some place where he would live by himself without help from anyone until he died again.

At one point I became so fearful of this dream that I tried not to go to sleep. I tried to think of good things about my father and to remember him before his illness. He used to call me "matey." "Hello, matey," he would say when he came home from work. He always wanted us to go someplace—to the store, to the park, to a ball game. He loved to walk. When I went walking with him he would say: "Hold your shoulders back, don't slump. Hold your head up and look at the world. Walk as if you meant it!" As he strode down the street his shoulders moved from side to side, as if he was hearing some kind of cakewalk. He moved with a bounce. He was always eager to see what was around the corner.

THE NEXT REQUEST for a letter coincided with a special occasion in the house: My brother Harold had met a girl he liked and had gone out with her several times. Now she was coming to our house for dinner.

We had prepared for this for days, cleaning everything in sight, giving the house a going-over, washing the dust of disuse from the glasses and good dishes. My mother came home early from work to get the dinner going. We opened the gateleg table in the living room and brought in the kitchen chairs. My mother spread the table with a laundered white cloth and put out her silver. It was the first family occasion since my father's illness.

I liked my brother's girlfriend a lot. She was a thin girl with very straight hair and she had a terrific smile. Her presence seemed to excite the air. It was amazing to have a living breathing girl in our house. She looked around and what she said was: "Oh, I've never seen so many books!" While she and my brother sat at the table my mother was in the kitchen putting the food into serving bowls and I was going from the kitchen to the living room, kidding around like a waiter, with a white cloth over my arm and a high style of service, placing the serving dish of green beans on the

table with a flourish. In the kitchen my mother's eyes were spar-
kling. She looked at me and nodded and mimed the words: "She's
adorable!"

My brother suffered himself to be waited on. He was wary of what
we might say. He kept glancing at the girl—her name was Susan—
to see if we met with her approval. She worked in an insurance office
and was taking courses in accounting at City College. Harold was
under a terrible strain but he was excited and happy too. He had
bought a bottle of Concord-grape wine to go with the roast chicken.
He held up his glass and proposed a toast. My mother said: "To good
health and happiness," and we all drank, even I. At that moment the
phone rang and I went into the bedroom to get it.

"Jonathan? This is your Aunt Frances. How is everyone?"

"Fine, thank you."

"I want to ask one last favor of you. I need a letter from Jack. Your
grandma's very ill. Do you think you can?"

"Who is it?" my mother called from the living room.

"OK, Aunt Frances," I said quickly. "I have to go now, we're
eating dinner." And I hung up the phone.

"It was my friend Louie," I said, sitting back down. "He didn't
know the math pages to review."

The dinner was very fine. Harold and Susan washed the dishes
and by the time they were done my mother and I had folded up the
gateleg table and put it back against the wall and I had swept the
crumbs up with the carpet sweeper. We all sat and talked and listened to records for a while and then my brother took Susan home.
The evening had gone very well.

ONCE WHEN MY MOTHER wasn't home my brother had
pointed out something: the letters from Jack weren't really necessary. "What is this ritual?" he said, holding his palms up. "Grandma
is almost totally blind, she's half deaf and crippled. Does the situation

really call for a literary composition? Does it need verisimilitude? Would the old lady know the difference if she was read the phone book?"

"Then why did Aunt Frances ask me?"

"That is the question, Jonathan. Why did she? After all, she could write the letter herself—what difference would it make? And if not Frances, why not Frances' sons, the Amherst students? They should have learned by now to write."

"But they're not Jack's sons," I said.

"That's exactly the point," my brother said. "The idea is *service*. Dad used to bust his balls getting them things wholesale, getting them deals on things. Frances of Westchester really needed things at cost. And Aunt Molly. And Aunt Molly's husband, and Aunt Molly's ex-husband. Grandma, if she needed an errand done. He was always on the hook for something. They never thought his time was important. They never thought every favor he got was one he had to pay back. Appliances, records, watches, china, opera tickets, any goddamn thing. Call Jack."

"It was a matter of pride to him to be able to do things for them," I said. "To have connections."

"Yeah, I wonder why," my brother said. He looked out the window.

Then suddenly it dawned on me that I was being implicated.

"You should use your head more," my brother said.

YET I HAD AGREED once again to write a letter from the desert and so I did. I mailed it off to Aunt Frances. A few days later, when I came home from school, I thought I saw her sitting in her car in front of our house. She drove a black Buick Roadmaster, a very large clean car with whitewall tires. It was Aunt Frances all right. She blew the horn when she saw me. I went over and leaned in at the window.

"Hello, Jonathan," she said. "I haven't long. Can you get in the car?"

"Mom's not home," I said. "She's working."

"I know that. I came to talk to you."

"Would you like to come upstairs?"

"I can't, I have to get back to Larchmont. Can you get in for a moment, please?"

I got in the car. My Aunt Frances was a very pretty white-haired woman, very elegant, and she wore tasteful clothes. I had always liked her and from the time I was a child she had enjoyed pointing out to everyone that I looked more like her son than Jack's. She wore white gloves and held the steering wheel and looked straight ahead as she talked, as if the car was in traffic and not sitting at the curb.

"Jonathan," she said, "there is your letter on the seat. Needless to say I didn't read it to Grandma. I'm giving it back to you and I won't ever say a word to anyone. This is just between us. I never expected cruelty from you. I never thought you were capable of doing something so deliberately cruel and perverse."

I said nothing.

"Your mother has very bitter feelings and now I see she has poisoned you with them. She has always resented the family. She is a very strong-willed, selfish person."

"No she isn't," I said.

"I wouldn't expect you to agree. She drove poor Jack crazy with her demands. She always had the highest aspirations and he could never fulfill them to her satisfaction. When he still had his store he kept your mother's brother, who drank, on salary. After the war when he began to make a little money he had to buy Ruth a mink jacket because she was so desperate to have one. He had debts to pay but she wanted a mink. He was a very special person, my brother, he should have accomplished something special, but he loved your mother and devoted his life to her. And all she ever thought about was keeping up with the Joneses."

I watched the traffic going up the Grand Concourse. A bunch of kids were waiting at the bus stop at the corner. They had put their books on the ground and were horsing around.

"I'm sorry I have to descend to this," Aunt Frances said. "I don't like talking about people this way. If I have nothing good to say about someone, I'd rather not say anything. How is Harold?"

"Fine."

"Did he help you write this marvelous letter?"

"No."

After a moment she said more softly: "How are you all getting along?"

"Fine."

"I would invite you up for Passover if I thought your mother would accept."

I didn't answer.

She turned on the engine. "I'll say good-bye now, Jonathan. Take your letter. I hope you give some time to thinking about what you've done."

THAT EVENING when my mother came home from work I saw that she wasn't as pretty as my Aunt Frances. I usually thought my mother was a good-looking woman, but I saw now that she was too heavy and that her hair was undistinguished.

"Why are you looking at me?" she said.

"I'm not."

"I learned something interesting today," my mother said. "We may be eligible for a V.A. pension because of the time your father spent in the Navy."

That took me by surprise. Nobody had ever told me my father was in the Navy.

"In World War I," she said, "he went to Webb's Naval Academy on the Harlem River. He was training to be an ensign. But the war ended and he never got his commission."

After dinner the three of us went through the closets looking for my father's papers, hoping to find some proof that could be filed with the Veterans Administration. We came up with two things, a Victory medal, which my brother said everyone got for being in the service during the Great War, and an astounding sepia photograph of my father and his shipmates on the deck of a ship. They were dressed in bell-bottoms and T-shirts and armed with mops and pails, brooms and brushes.

"I never knew this," I found myself saying. "I never knew this."

"You just don't remember," my brother said.

I was able to pick out my father. He stood at the end of the row, a thin, handsome boy with a full head of hair, a mustache, and an intelligent smiling countenance.

"He had a joke," my mother said. "They called their training ship the S.S. *Constipation* because it never moved."

Neither the picture nor the medal was proof of anything, but my brother thought a duplicate of my father's service record had to be in Washington somewhere and that it was just a matter of learning how to go about finding it.

"The pension wouldn't amount to much," my mother said. "Twenty or thirty dollars. But it would certainly help."

I took the picture of my father and his shipmates and propped it against the lamp at my bedside. I looked into his youthful face and tried to relate it to the Father I knew. I looked at the picture a long time. Only gradually did my eye connect it to the set of Great Sea Novels in the bottom shelf of the bookcase a few feet away. My father had given that set to me: it was uniformly bound in green with gilt lettering and it included works by Melville, Conrad, Victor Hugo and Captain Marryat. And lying across the top of the books, jammed in under the sagging shelf above, was his old ship's telescope in its wooden case with the brass snap.

I thought how stupid, and imperceptive, and self-centered I had been never to have understood while he was alive what my father's dream for his life had been.

On the other hand, I had written in my last letter from Arizona —the one that had so angered Aunt Frances—something that might allow me, the writer in the family, to soften my judgment of myself. I will conclude by giving the letter here in its entirety.

Dear Mama,

This will be my final letter to you since I have been told by the doctors that I am dying.

I have sold my store at a very fine profit and am sending Frances a check for five thousand dollars to be deposited in your account. My present to you, Mamaleh. Let Frances show you the passbook.

As for the nature of my ailment, the doctors haven't told me what it is, but I know that I am simply dying of the wrong life. I should never have come to the desert. It wasn't the place for me.

I have asked Ruth and the boys to have my body cremated and the ashes scattered in the ocean.

Your loving son,
Jack

THE
WATER
WORKS

□   □   □

I HAD FOLLOWED my man here. Everything he did was mysterious to me, and his predilection for the Water Works this November day was no less so. A square, granite building, with crenelated turrets at the corners, it stood hard by the reservoir on a high plain overlooking the city from the north. There was an abundance of windows through which, however, no light seemed to pass. I saw reflected the sky behind me, a tumultuous thing of billowing shapes of gray tumbling through vaults of pink sunset and with black rain clouds sailing overhead like an armada.

His carriage was in the front yard. His horse pawed the stony ground and swung its head about to look at me.

The reservoir behind the building, five or six city blocks in area, was cratered in an embankment that went up from the ground at an angle suggesting the pyramidal platform of an ancient civilization, Mayan perhaps. On Sundays in warm weather, people came here from the city and climbed the embankment, calling out to one another as they rose to the sight of a squared expanse of water. This day it was his alone. I heard the violent chop, the insistent slap of the tides against the cobblestone.

He stood a ways out in the darkening day; he was studying

something upon the water, my black-bearded captain. He held his hat brim. The corner of his long coat took the wind and pressed against his leg.

I was sure he knew of my presence. Indeed, for some days I had sensed from his actions a mad presumption of partnership, as if he engaged in his enterprises for our mutual benefit. I climbed the embankment a hundred or so yards to his east and faced into the wind to see the object of his attention.

It was a toy boat under sail, rising and falling in heavy swells at alarming heel, disappearing and then reappearing all atumble, water pouring off her sides.

We watched her for several minutes. She disappeared and rose and again disappeared. There was a rhythm in this to lull the perception, and some moments passed before I realized, waiting for her rising, that I waited in vain. I was as struck in the chest with the catastrophe as if I had stood on some cliff and watched the sea take a sailing vessel.

When I thought to look for my man, he was running across the wide moat of hardened earth that led to the rear gates of the Water Works. I followed. Inside the building I felt the chill of entombed air and I heard the orchestra of water hissing and roaring in its fall. I ran down a stone corridor and found another that offered passage to the left or right. I listened. I heard his steps clearly, a metallic rap of heels echoing from my right. At the end of the dark conduit was a flight of iron stairs rising circularly about a black steel gear shaft. Around I went, rising, and reaching the top story, I found the view opening out from a catwalk over a vast inner pool of roiling water. This hellish churn pounded up a mineral mist, like a fifth element, in whose sustenance there grew on the blackened stone face of the far wall a profusion of moss and slime.

Above me was a skylight of translucent glass. By its dim light I discovered him not five feet from where I stood. He was bent over the rail with a rapt expression of the most awful intensity. I thought he would topple, so unaware of himself did he seem in that moment. I found the sight of him in his passion almost unendurable. So again I looked at what he was seeing, and there below, in the yellowing rush of spumed currents and water plunging into its mechanical harness, a small human body was pressed against the machinery of one of the sluicegates, its clothing caught as in some hinge, and the child, for it was a miniature like the ship in the reservoir, went slamming about, first one way and then the next, as if in mute protest, trembling and shaking and animating by its revulsion the death that had already overtaken it. Someone shouted, and after a moment I saw, as if they had separated from the stone, three uniformed men poised on a lower ledge. They were well apprised of the situation. They were heaving on a line strung from a pulley fixed in the far wall, and by this means advancing a towline attached to the wall below my catwalk where I could not see. But now into view he came, another of the water workers, suspended from a sling by the ankles, his hands outstretched as he waited to be aligned so that he could free the flow of this obstruction.

And then he had him, raised from the water by his shirt, an urchin, anywhere from four to eight I would have said, drowned blue, and then by the ankles and shoes; and so suspended, both, they swung back across the pouring currents rhythmically, like performing aerialists, till they were out of sight below me.

I wondered, perhaps from the practiced quality of their maneuver, if the water workers were not accustomed to such impediments. A few minutes later, in the yard under the darkened sky, I watched my man load the wrapped corpse into his carriage, shut the door smartly, and leap then to the high seat, where he commanded his horse with a great rolling snap of the reins. And off it went, the bright black wheel spokes brought to a blur as the dead child was raced to the city.

The rain had begun. I went back in and felt the oppression of a universe of water, inside and out, over the dead and the living.

The water workers were dividing some treasure among themselves. They wore the dark-blue uniform with the high collar of the city employee, but amended with rough sweaters under the tunics and with trousers tucked into their high boots. It was not an enviable employment here. I could imagine in human lungs the same flora that grew on stone. Their faces were bright and flushed, their blood urged to the skin by the chill and their skin brought to a high glaze by the mist.

They saw me and made a great show of not caring. They broke out the whiskey for their tin cups. There is such a cherishing of ritual too among firemen and gravediggers.

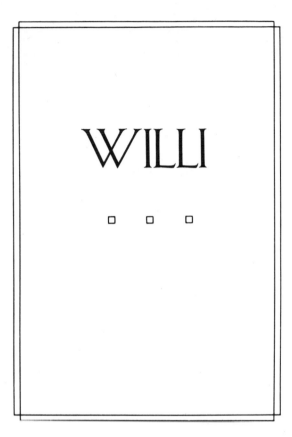

WILLI

□   □   □

O NE SPRING DAY I walked in the meadow behind the barn and felt rising around me the exhalations of the field, the moist sweetness of the grasses, and I imagined the earth's soul lifting to the warmth of the sun and mingling me in some divine embrace. There was such brilliant conviction in the colors of the golden hay meadow, the blue sky, that I could not help laughing. I threw myself down in the grass and spread my arms. I fell at once into a trance and yet remained incredibly aware, so that whatever I opened my eyes to look at I did not merely see but felt as its existence. Such states come naturally to children. I was resonant with the hum of the universe, I was made indistinguishable from the world in a great bonding of natural revelation. I saw the drowse of gnats weaving between the grasses and leaving infinitesimally fine threads of shimmering net, so highly textured that the breath of the soil below lifted it in gentle billows. Minute crawling life on the stalks of hay made colossal odyssey, journeys of a lifetime, before my eyes. Yet there was no thought of miracle, of the miracle of microscopic sentience. The scale of the universe was not pertinent, and the smallest indications of energy were in proportion to the sun, which lay like an Egyptian eye between the stalks, and lit them as it lights the earth, by halves. The hay had fallen under me so that my own body's outline was patterned on the field, the outspread legs and arms, the fingers, and I was aware of my being as the arbitrary shape of an agency that had chosen to make me in this manner as a means of communicating with me. The very idea of a head and limbs and a body was substantive only as an act of communication, and I felt myself in the prickle of the flattened grass, and the sense of imposition was now enormous, a prodding, a lifting of this part of the world that was for some reason my momentary responsibility, that was giving me possession of itself. And I rose and seemed to ride on the planes of the sun, which I felt in fine striations, alternated with thin lines of the earth's moist essences. And invisibled by my revelation, I reached the barn and examined the face of it, standing with my face in the painted whiteness of its glare as a dog or a cat stands nose to a door until someone comes and lets it out. And I moved along the white barn wall, sidestepping until I came to the window which was a simple square without glass, and could only be felt by the geometrical coolness of its volume of inner air, for it was black within. And there I stood, as if in the mouth of a vacuum, and felt the insubstantial being of the sun meadow pulled past me into the barn, like a torrential implosion of light into darkness and life into death, and I myself too disintegrated in that force and was sucked like the chaff of the field in that roaring. Yet I stood where I was. And in quite normal spatial relationship with my surroundings felt the sun's quiet warmth on my back and the coolness of the cool barn on my face. And the windy universal roar in my ears had narrowed and refined itself to a recognizable frequency, that of a woman's pulsating song in the act of love, the gasp and note and gasp and note of an ecstatic score. I listened. And pressed upon by the sun, as if it were a hand on the back of my neck, I moved my face into the portal of the cool darkness, and no longer blinded by the sunlight, my eyes saw on the straw and in the dung my mother, denuded, in a pose of utmost degradation, a body, a reddened headless body, the head enshrouded in her clothing, everything turned inside out, as if blown out by the wind, all order, truth, and reason, and this defiled mama played violently upon and being made to sing her defilement. How can I describe what I felt! I felt I deserved to see this! I felt it was my triumph, but I felt monstrously betrayed. I felt drained suddenly of the strength to stand. I turned my back and slid down the wall to a sitting position under the window. My heart in my chest banged in sickened measure of her cries. I wanted to kill him, this killer of my mother who was killing her. I wanted to leap through the window and drive a pitchfork into his back, but I wanted him to be killing her, I wanted him to be killing her for me. I wanted to be him. I lay on the ground, and with my arms over my head and my hands clasped and my ankles locked, I rolled down the slope behind the barn, through the grass and the crop of hay. I flattened the hay like a mechanical cylinder of irrepressible force rolling fast and faster over rocks, through rivulets, across furrows and over hummocks of the uneven imperfect flawed irregular earth, the sun flashing in my closed eyes in diurnal emergency, as if time and the planet had gone out of control. As it has. (I am recalling these things now, a man older than my father when he died, and to whom a woman of my mother's age when all this happened is a young woman barely half my age. What an incredible achievement of fantasy is the scientific mind! We posit an empirical world, yet how can I be here at this desk in this room—and not be here? If memory is a matter of the stimulation of so many cells of the brain, the greater the stimulus— remorse, the recognition of fate—the more powerfully complete becomes the sensation of the memory until there is transfer, as in a time machine, and the memory is in the ontological sense another reality.) Papa, I see you now in the universe of your own making. I walk the polished floorboards of your house and seat myself at your dining table. I feel the tassels of the tablecloth on the tops of my bare

knees. The light of the candelabra shines on your smiling mouth of
big teeth. I notice the bulge of your neck produced by your shirt
collar. Your pink scalp is visible through the close-cropped German-
style haircut. I see your head raised in conversation and your white
plump hand of consummate gesture making its point to your wife
at the other end of the table. Mama is so attentive. The candle flame
burns in her eyes and I imagine the fever there, but she is quite calm
and seriously engrossed by what you say. Her long neck, very white,
is hung with a thin chain from which depends on the darkness of
her modest dress a cream-colored cameo, the carved profile of another fine lady of another time. In her neck a soft slow pulse beats.
Her small hands are folded and the bones of her wrists emerge from
the touch of lace at her cuffs. She is smiling at you in your loving
proprietorship, proud of you, pleased to be yours, and the mistress
of this house, and the mother of this boy. Of my tutor across the table
from me who idly twirls the stem of his wineglass and glances at her,
she is barely aware. Her eyes are for her husband. I think now Papa
her feelings in this moment are sincere. I know now each moment
has its belief and what we call treachery is the belief of each moment,
the wish for it to be as it seems to be. It is possible in joy to love the
person you have betrayed and to be refreshed in your love for him,
it is entirely possible. Love renews all faces and customs and ideals
and leaves the bars of the prison shining. But how could a boy know
that? I ran to my room and waited for someone to follow me.
Whoever dared to enter my room, I would attack—would pummel.
I wanted it to be her, I wanted her to come to me, to hug me and
to hold my head and kiss me on the lips as she liked to do, I wanted
her to make those wordless sounds of comfort as she held me to her
when I was hurt or unhappy, and when she did that I would beat
her with my fists, beat her to the floor, and see her raise her hands
helplessly in terror as I beat her and kicked her and jumped upon
her and drove the breath from her body. But it was my tutor who,

sometime later, opened the door, looked in with his hand upon the knob, smiled, said a few words, and wished me good night. He closed the door and I heard him walk up the steps to the next floor, where he had his rooms. Ledig was his name. He was a Christian. I had looked but could not find in his face any sign of smugness or leering pride or cruelty. There was nothing coarse about him, nothing that could possibly give me offense. He was barely twenty. I even thought I saw in his eyes a measure of torment. He was habitually melancholic anyway, and during my lessons his mind often wandered and he would gaze out the window and sigh. He was as much a schoolboy as his pupil. So there was every reason to refrain from judgment, to let time pass, to think, to gain understanding. Nobody knew that I knew. I had that choice. But did I? They had made my position intolerable. I was given double vision, the kind that comes with a terrible blow. I found I could not have anything to do with my kind sweet considerate mother. I found I could not bear the gentle pedagogics of my tutor. How, in that rural isolation, could I be expected to go on? I had no friends, I was not permitted to play with the children of the peasants who worked for us. I had only this trinity of Mother and Tutor and Father, this unholy trinity of deception and ignorance who had excommunicated me from my life at the age of thirteen. This of course in the calendar of traditional Judaism is the year a boy enjoys his initiation into manhood.

Meanwhile my father was going about the triumph of his life, running a farm according to the most modern principles of scientific management, astonishing his peasants and angering the other farmers in the region with his success. The sun brought up his crops, the Galician Agricultural Society gave him an award for the quality of his milk, and he lived in the state of abiding satisfaction given to individuals who are more than a match for the life they have chosen for themselves. I had incorporated him into the universe of giant powers that I, a boy, experienced in the changes of the seasons. I watched bulls bred to cows, watched mares foal, I saw life come from the egg and the multiplicative wonders of mudholes and ponds, the jell and slime of life shimmering in gravid expectation. Everywhere I looked, life sprang from something not life, insects unfolded from sacs on the surface of still waters and were instantly on the prowl for their dinner, everything that came into being knew at once what to do and did it unastonished that it was what it was, unimpressed by where it was, the great earth heaving up its bloodied newborns from every pore, every cell, bearing the variousness of itself from every conceivable substance which it contained in itself, sprouting life that flew or waved in the wind or blew from the mountains or stuck to the damp black underside of rocks, or swam or suckled or bellowed or silently separated in two. I placed my father in all of this as the owner and manager. He lived in the universe of giant powers by understanding it and making it serve him, using the daily sun for his crops and breeding what naturally bred, and so I distinguished him in it as the god-eye in the kingdom, the intelligence that brought order and gave everything its value. He loved me and I can still feel my pleasure in making him laugh, and I might not be deceiving myself when I remember the feel on my infant hand of his unshaved cheek, the winy smell of his breath, the tobacco smoke in his thick wavy hair, or his mock-wondering look of foolish happiness during our play together. He had close-set eyes, the color of dark grapes, that opened wide in our games. He would laugh like a horse and show large white teeth. He was a strong man, stocky and powerful —the constitution I inherited—and he had emerged as an orphan from the alleys of cosmopolitan eastern Europe, like Darwin's amphibians from the sea, and made himself a landowner, a husband and father. He was a Jew who spoke no Yiddish and a farmer raised in the city. I was not allowed to play with village children, or to go to their crude schools. We lived alone, isolated on our estate, neither Jew nor Christian, neither friend nor petitioner of the Austro-Hungarians, but in the pride of the self-constructed self. To this day I don't know how he arranged it or what hungering rage had caused him to deny every classification society imposes and to live as an anomaly, tied to no past in a world which, as it happened, had no future. But I am in awe that he did it. Because he stood up in his life he was exposed to the swords of Mongol horsemen, the scythes of peasants in revolution, the lowered brows of monstrous bankers and the cruciform gestures of prelates. His arrogance threatened him with the cumulative power of all of European history which was ready to take his head, nail it to a pole and turn him into one of the scarecrows in his fields, arms held stiffly out toward life. But when the moment came for this transformation, it was accomplished quite easily, by a word from his son. I was the agency of his downfall. Ancestry and myth, culture, history and time were ironically composed in the shape of his own boy.

I WATCHED HER for several days. I remembered the rash of passion on her flesh. I was so ashamed of myself that I felt continuously ill, and it was the vaguest, most diffuse nausea, nausea of the blood, nausea of the bone. In bed at night I found it difficult breathing, and terrible waves of fever broke over me and left me parched in my terror. I couldn't purge from my mind the image of her overthrown body, the broad whitenesses, her shoed feet in the air; I made her scream ecstatically every night in my dreams and awoke one dawn in my own sap. That was the crisis that toppled me, for in fear of being found out by the maid and by my mother, for fear of being found out by them all as the archcriminal of my dreams, I ran to him, I went to him for absolution, I confessed and put myself at his mercy. Papa, I said. He was down by the kennels mating a pair of vizslas. He used this breed to hunt. He had rigged some sort of harness for the bitch so that she could not bolt, a kind of pillory, and she was putting up a terrible howl, and though her tail showed her amenable, she moved her rump away from the proddings of the erect male, who mounted and pumped and missed and mounted again and couldn't hold her still. My father was banging the fist of his right hand into the palm of his left. Put it to her, he shouted, come on, get it in there, give it to her. Then the male had success and the mating began, the female standing there quietly now, sweat dripping off her chops, an occasional groan escaping from her. And then the male came, and stood front paws on her back, his tongue lolling as he panted, and they waited as dogs do for the detumescence. My father knelt beside them and soothed them with quiet words. Good dogs, he said, good dogs. You must guard them at this time, he said to me, they try to uncouple too early and hurt themselves. Papa, I said. He turned and looked at me over his shoulder as he knelt beside the dogs, and I saw his happiness, and the glory of him in his work-pants tucked into a black pair of riding boots and his shirt open at the collar and the black hair of his chest curled as high as the throat, and I said, Papa, they should be named Mama and Ledig. And then I turned so quickly I do not even remember his face changing, I did not even wait to see if he understood me, I turned and ran, but I am sure of this—he never called after me.

There was a sun room in our house, a kind of conservatory with a glass outer wall and slanted ceiling of green glass framed in steel. It was a very luxurious appointment in that region, and it was my mother's favorite place to be. She had filled it with plants and books, and she liked to lie on a chaise in this room and read and smoke cigarettes. I found her there, as I knew I would, and I gazed at her with wonder and fascination because I knew her fate. She was in-credibly beautiful, with her dark hair parted in the center and tied behind her in a bun, and her small hands, and the lovely fullness of her chin, the indications under her chin of some fattening, like a quality of indolence in her character. But a man would not dwell on this as on her neck, so lovely and slim, or the high modestly dressed bosom. A man would not want to see signs of the future. Since she was my mother it had never occurred to me how many years younger she was than my father. He had married her out of the gymnasium; she was the eldest of four daughters and her parents had been eager to settle her in prosperous welfare, which is what a mature man offers. It is not that the parents are unaware of the erotic component for the man in this sort of marriage. They are fully aware of it. Rectitude, propriety, are always very practical. I gazed at her in wonder and awe. I blushed. What? she said. She put her book down and smiled and held out her arms. What, Willi, what is it? I fell into her arms and began to sob and she held me and my tears wet the dark dress she wore. She held my head and whispered, What, Willi, what did you do to yourself, poor Willi? Then, aware that my sobs had become breathless and hysterical, she held me at arm's length—tears and snot were dribbling from me—and her eyes widened in genuine alarm.

That night I heard from the bedroom the shocking exciting sounds of her undoing. I have heard such terrible sounds of blows upon a body in Berlin after the war, Freikorps hoodlums in the streets attacking whores they had dragged from the brothel and tearing the clothes from their bodies and beating them to the cobblestones. I sat up in bed, hardly able to breathe, terrified, but feeling undeniable arousal. Give it to her, I muttered, banging my fist in my palm. Give it to her. But then I could bear it no longer and ran into their room and stood between them, lifting my screaming mother from the bed, holding her in my arms, shouting at my father to stop, to stop. But he reached around me and grabbed her hair with one hand and punched her face with the other. I was enraged, I pushed her back and jumped at him, pummeling him, shouting that I would kill him. This was in Galicia in the year 1910. All of it was to be destroyed anyway, even without me.

THE
HUNTER

□   □   □

T HE TOWN is terraced in the hill, along the river, a factory town of clapboard houses and public buildings faced in red stone. There is a one-room library called the Lyceum. There are several taverns made from porched homes, Miller and Bud signs hanging in neon in the front windows. Down at water's edge sits the old brassworks, a long two-story brick building with a tower at one end and it is behind locked fences and many of its windows are broken. The river is frozen. The town is dusted in new snow. Along the sides of the streets the winter's accumulated snow is banked high as a man's shoulder. Smoke drifts from the chimneys of the houses and is quickly sucked into the sky. The wind comes up off the river and sweeps up the hill through the houses.

A school bus makes its way through the narrow hill streets. The mothers and fathers stand on the porches above to watch the bus accept their children. It's the only thing moving in the town. The fathers fill their arms with firewood stacked by the front doors and go back inside. Trees are black in the woods behind the homes; they are black against the snow. Sparrow and finch dart from branch to branch and puff their feathers to keep warm. They flutter to the ground and hop on the snow-crust under the trees.

The children enter the school through the big oak doors with the push bars. It is not a large school but its proportions, square and high, create hollow rooms and echoing stairwells. The children sit in their rows with their hands folded and watch their teacher. She is cheery and kind. She has been here just long enough for her immodest wish to transform these children to have turned to awe at what they are. Their small faces have been rubbed raw by the cold; the weakness of their fair skin is brought out in blotches on their cheeks and in the blue pallor of their eyelids. Their eyelids are translucent membranes, so thin and so delicate that she wonders how they sleep, how they keep from seeing through their closed eyes.

She tells them she is happy to see them here in such cold weather, with a hard wind blowing up the valley and another storm coming. She begins the day's work with their exercise, making them squat and bend and jump and swing their arms and somersault so that they can see what the world looks like upside down. How does it look? she cries, trying it herself, somersaulting on the gym mat until she's dizzy.

They are not animated but the exercise alerts them to the mood she's in. They watch her with interest to see what is next. She leads them out of the small, dimly lit gymnasium through the empty halls, up and down the stairs, telling them they are a lost patrol in the caves of a planet somewhere far out in space. They are looking for signs of life. They wander through the unused schoolrooms, where crayon drawings hang from one thumbtack and corkboards have curled away from their frames. Look, she calls, holding up a child's red rubber boot, fished from the depths of a classroom closet. You never can tell!

When they descend to the basement, the janitor dozing in his cubicle is startled awake by a group of children staring at him. He is a large bearish man and wears fatigue pants and a red plaid woolen shirt. The teacher has never seen him wear anything different. His face has a gray stubble. We're a lost patrol, she says to him, have you seen any living creatures hereabouts? The janitor frowns. What? he says. What?

It is warm in the basement. The furnace emits its basso roar. She has him open the furnace door so the children can see the source of heat, the fire in its pit. They are each invited to cast a handful of coal through the door. They do this as a sacrament.

Then she insists that the janitor open the storage rooms and the old lunchroom kitchen, and here she notes unused cases of dried soup mix and canned goods, and then large pots and thick aluminum cauldrons and a stack of metal trays with food compartments. Here, you can't take those, the janitor says. And why not, she answers, this is their school, isn't it? She gives each child a tray or pot, and they march upstairs, banging them with their fists to scare away the creatures of wet flesh and rotating eyes and pulpy horns who may be lying in wait round the corners.

In the afternoon it is already dark, and the school bus receives the children in the parking lot behind the building. The new street lamps installed by the county radiate an amber light. The yellow school bus in the amber light is the color of a dark egg yolk. As it leaves, the children, their faces indistinct behind the windows, turn to stare out at the young teacher. She waves, her fingers opening and closing like a fluttering wing. The bus windows slide past, breaking her image and re-forming it, and giving her the illusion of the stone building behind her sliding along its foundations in the opposite direction.

The bus has turned into the road. It goes slowly past the school. The children's heads lurch in unison as the driver shifts gears. The bus plunges out of sight in the dip of the hill. At this moment the teacher realizes that she did not recognize the driver. He was not the small, burly man with eyeglasses without rims. He was a young man with long light hair and white eyebrows, and he looked at her in the instant he hunched over the steering wheel, with his arms about to make the effort of putting the bus into a turn.

THAT EVENING at home the young woman heats water for a bath and pours it in the tub. She bathes and urinates in the bathwater. She brings her hands out of the water and lets it pour through her fingers. She hums a made-up tune. The bathroom is large, with wainscoting of wood strips painted gray. The tub rests on four cast-iron claws. A small window high on the wall is open just a crack and through it the night air sifts into the room. She lies back and the cold air comes along the water line and draws its finger across her neck.

In the morning she dresses and combs her hair back and ties it behind her head and wears small opal teardrop earrings given to her for her graduation from college. She walks to work, opens up the school, turns up the radiator, cleans the blackboard, and goes to the front door to await the children on the yellow bus.

They do not come.

She goes to her teaching room, rearranges the day's lesson on the desk, distributes a sheet of stiff paper to each child's desk. She goes back to the front door and awaits the children.

They are nowhere in sight.

She looks for the school janitor in the basement. The furnace makes a kind of moaning sound, there is rhythmic intensification of its running pitch, and he's staring at it with a perplexed look on his face. He tells her the time, and it is the time on her watch. She goes back upstairs and stands at the front door with her coat on.

The yellow bus comes into the school driveway and pulls up before the front door. She puts her hand on the shoulder of each child descending the steps from the bus. The young man with the blond hair and eyebrows smiles at her.

There have been sacred rites and legendary events in this town. In a semi-pro football game a player was killed. A presidential candidate once came and spoke. A mass funeral was held here for the victims of a shoe-factory fire. She understands the new bus driver has no knowledge of any of this.

ON SATURDAY MORNING the teacher goes to the old people's home and reads aloud. They sit there and listen to the story. They are the children's faces in another time. She thinks she can even recognize some of the grandmothers and grandfathers by family. When the reading is over those who can walk come up to her and pluck at her sleeves and her collar, interrupting each other to tell her who they are and what they used to be. They shout at each other. They mock each other's words. They waggle their hands in her face to get her to look at them.

She cannot get out of there fast enough. In the street she breaks into a run. She runs until the old people's home is out of sight.

It is very cold, but the sun shines. She decides to walk up to the mansion at the top of the highest hill in town. The hill streets turn abruptly back on themselves like a series of chutes. She wears lace-up boots and jeans. She climbs through snowdrifts in which she sinks up to the thighs.

The old mansion sits in the sun above the tree line. It is said that one of the factory owners built it for his bride, and that shortly after taking possession he killed her with a shotgun. The Greek columns have great chunks missing and she sees chicken wire exposed under the plaster. The portico is hung with icicles, and snow is backed against the house. There is no front door. She goes in. The light of the sun and a fall of snow fill the entrance hall and its grand stairway. She can see the sky through the collapsed ceiling and a crater in the roof. She moves carefully and goes to the door of what must have been the dining room. She opens it. It smells of rot. There is a rustle and a hissing sound and she sees several pairs of eyes constellated in the dark. She opens the door wider. Many cats are backed into a corner of the room. They growl at her and twitch their tails.

She goes out and walks around to the back, an open field white in the sun. There is a pitted aluminum straight ladder leaning against a windowsill in the second floor. She climbs the ladder. The window is punched out and she climbs through the frame and stands in a light and airy bedroom. A hemisphere of ice hangs from the ceiling. It looks like the bottom of the moon. She stands at the window and sees at the edge of the field a man in an orange jacket and red hat. She wonders if he can see her from this distance. He raises a rifle to his shoulder and a moment later she hears an odd smack as if someone has hit the siding of the house with an open palm. She does not move. The hunter lowers his rifle and steps back into the woods at the edge of the field.

T H A T　E V E N I N G　the young teacher calls the town physician to ask for something to take. What seems to be the trouble? the doctor says. She conceives of a self-deprecating answer, sounding confident and assertive, even managing a small laugh. He says he will call the druggist and prescribe Valiums, two-milligram so that she won't be made drowsy by them. She walks down to Main Street, where the druggist opens his door and without turning on the store light leads her to the prescription counter in the rear. The druggist puts his hand into a large jar and comes up with a handful of tablets, and feeds the Valium one by one, from his thumb and forefinger, into a vial.

She goes to the movie theater on Main Street and pays her admission. The theater bears the same name as the town. She sits in the dark and swallows a handful of tabs. She cannot discern the picture. The screen is white. Then what she sees forming on the white screen is the town in its blanket of snow, the clapboard houses on the hill, the frozen river, the wind blowing snow along the streets. She sees the children coming out of their doors with their schoolbooks and walking down their steps to the street. She sees her life exactly as it is outside the movie theater.

Later she walks through the downtown. The only thing open is the State News. Several men stand thumbing the magazines. She turns down Mechanic Street and walks past the tool-and-die company and crosses the railroad tracks to the bridge. She begins to run. In the middle of the bridge the wind is a force and she feels it wants to press her through the railing into the river. She runs bent over, feeling as if she is pushing through something, as if it is only giving way to her by tearing.

Across the bridge the road turns sharply left and at the curve, at the foot of a hill of pine trees, is a brown house with a neon sign in the window: The Rapids. She climbs up the porch steps into the Rapids, and looking neither left nor right, walks to the back, where she finds the ladies' room. When she comes out she sits in one of the varnished plywood booths and stares at the table. After a while a man in an apron comes over and she orders a beer. Only then does she look up. The light is dim. A couple of elderly men are at the bar. But alone down at the end, established with his glass and a pack of cigarettes, is the new bus driver with the long blond hair, and he is smiling at her.

HE HAS joined her. For a while nothing is said. He raises his arm and turns in his seat to look toward the bar. He turns his head to look back at her. You want another, he says. She shakes her head no but doesn't say thank you. She digs in her coat pocket and puts a wrinkled dollar beside her bottle. He holds up one finger.

You from around here? he says.

From the eastern part of the state, she says.

I'm from Valdese, he says. Down on Sixteen.

Oh yes.

I know you're their teacher, he says. I'm their driver.

He wears a wool shirt and a denim jacket and jeans. It is what he wears in his bus. He would not own a coat. There is something on a chain around his neck but it is hidden under the shirt. Blond beard stubble lies sparsely on his chin and along the line of his jaw. His cheeks are smooth. He is smiling. One of his front teeth is chipped.

What do you do to get to be a teacher?

You go to college. She sighs: What do you do to be a driver?

It's a county job, he says. You need a chauffeur's license and a clean record.

What is a dirty record?

Why, if you been arrested, you know? If you have any kind of record. Or if you got a bad service discharge.

She waits.

I had a teacher once in the third grade, he says. I believe she was the most beautiful woman I have ever seen. I believe now she was no more'n a girl. Like you. But she was very proud and she had a way of tossing her head and walking that made me wish to be a better student.

She laughs.

He picks up her beer bottle and feigns reproach and holds up his arm to the bartender and signals for two.

It is very easy, she says, to make them fall in love with you. Boys or girls, it's very easy.

And to herself she admits that she tries to do it, to make them love her, she takes on a grace she doesn't really have at any other time. She moves like a dancer, she touches them and brushes against them. She is outgoing and shows no terror, and the mystery of her is created in their regard.

Do you have sisters? she says.

Two. How'd you know that?

They're older than you?

One older, one younger.

What do they do?

Work in the office of the lumber mill down there.

She says: I would trust a man who had sisters.

He tilts his head back and takes a long pull at his beer bottle, and she watches his Adam's apple rise and fall, and the sparse blond stubble on his throat move like reeds lying on the water.

Later they come out of the Rapids and he leads her to his pickup. He is rather short. She climbs in and notices his workboots when he comes up into the cab from the other side. They're clean good boots, new yellow leather. He has trouble starting the engine.

What are you doing here at night if you live in Valdese? she says.

Waiting for you. He laughs and the engine turns over.

They drive slowly across the bridge, and across the tracks. Following her instructions, he goes to the end of the main street and turns up into the hills and brings her to her house. He pulls up in the yard by the side door.

It is a small house and it looks dark and cold. He switches off the engine and the headlights and leans across her lap and presses the button of the glove compartment. He says: Happens I got me some party wine right here. He removes a flat bottle in a brown bag and slams the door, and as he moves back, his arm brushes her thigh.

She stares through the windshield. She says: Stupid goddamn mill hand. Making his play with the teacher. Look at that, with his party wine in a sack. I can't believe it.

She jumps down from the cab, runs around the truck, and up the back steps into her kitchen. She slams the door. There is silence. She waits in the kitchen, not moving, in the dark, standing behind the table, facing the door.

She hears nothing but her own breathing.

All at once the back door is flooded with light, the white curtain on the door glass becomes a white screen, and then the light fades, and she hears the pickup backing out to the street. She is panting and now her rage breaks, and she is crying.

She stands alone in her dark kitchen crying, a bitter scent coming off her body, a smell of burning, which offends her. She heats water on the stove and takes it up to her bath.

O N   M O N D A Y   M O R N I N G   the teacher waits for her children at the front door of the school. When the bus turns into the drive, she steps back and stands inside the door. She can see the open door of the bus but she cannot see if he is trying to see her.

She is very animated this morning. This is a special day, children, she announces, and she astonishes them by singing them a song while she accompanies herself on the Autoharp. She lets them strum the Autoharp while she presses the chords. Look, she says to each one, you are making music.

At eleven the photographer arrives. He is a man with a potbelly and a black string tie. I don't get these school calls till spring, he says.

This is a special occasion, the teacher says. We want a picture of ourselves now. Don't we, children?

They watch intently as he sets up his tripod and camera. He has a black valise with brass latches that snap as he opens them. Inside are cables and floodlamps.

Used to be classes of kids, he says. Now look at what's left of you. Heat this whole building for one room.

By the time he is ready, the young teacher has pushed the benches to the blackboard and grouped the children in two rows, the taller ones sitting on the benches, the shorter ones sitting in front of them on the floor, cross-legged. She herself stands at one side. There are fifteen children staring at the camera and their smiling teacher holding her hands in front of her, like an opera singer.

The photographer looks at the scene and frowns. Why, these children ain't fixed up for their picture.

What do you mean?

Why, they ain't got on their ties and their new shoes. You got girls here wearing trousers.

Just take it, she says.

They don't look right. Their hair ain't combed, these boys here.

Take us as we are, the teacher says. She steps suddenly out of line and with a furious motion removes the barrette fastening her hair and shakes her head until her hair falls to her shoulders. The children are startled. She kneels down on the floor in front of them, facing the camera, and pulls two of them into her arms. She brings all of them around her with an urgent opening and closing of her hands, and they gather about her. One girl begins to cry.

She pulls them in around her, feeling their bodies, the thin bones of their arms, their small shoulders, their legs, their behinds.

Take it, she says in a fierce whisper. Take it as we are. We are looking at you. Take it.

THE
FOREIGN
LEGATION

□ □ □

A FTER HIS WIFE left with all her clothes and the children's clothes and toys, Morgan continued to go to work and come home, though the house was empty and he had no one to talk to.

In the evenings he stood at his windows with binoculars and watched the passage of his neighbors through their rooms.

Outside, in the twilight, featureless crows flapped from the maples to the tall pines or dropped to the pavement to peck at crumpled junk-food wrappers left by passing children.

This was a formal neighborhood in an old suburb. The houses were English Cottage or Dutch Colonial or Florentine Villa, all of them built in the twenties and thirties.

He took up running in the very early morning, when the lawns were webbed with dew and the dogs had not been let out.

He ran on streets of huge maples whose branches arched into high green vaults of sunlight.

He ran the winding streets of English, Dutch, and Florentine homes with their great trees and large yards, and then, as the streets straightened, through the newer neighborhoods of tract houses and

small ornamental trees and basketball backboards mounted over ga-
rage doors.

On Saturdays he drove to the shopping center. He bought expen-
sive steaks he would put in the freezer, and fruits and vegetables that
would go bad before he thought to eat them.

In the post office he mailed his bills and looked through the thick
bound book of Men Wanted notices chained to the customer
counter.

He knew there was nothing to keep him from changing his life,
but staying on suited his sense of himself as someone waiting.

He was waiting not for his wife and children, who he knew would
never come back, but for whatever it was he'd always waited.

If he read in the local paper, which he found neatly folded on his
porch each evening when he came home, that something had happened in his own or an adjoining neighborhood, that someone had
committed suicide or someone's teenage son or daughter had disappeared, the next morning he would run past the house where it
happened.

But he would see no sign that anything at all had happened. The
house was always quiet, the door closed, the car parked in the driveway.

Homes were for people's lives to explode in like those steel-mesh
hutches used by police bomb-disposal squads.

ONE MORNING Morgan ran farther than usual and came to the
open field that rose gradually to the red-stone Catholic girls' school.

Buses were letting out students before the flagpole in front of the
main entrance.

The students wore maroon knee socks and maroon plaid mini-
skirts and white long-sleeved blouses and they held their books
against their breasts.

Morgan did not go to work but in the afternoon drove to the

shopping center, where he saw students of that same school sitting at the counter in the Ice Cream Shoppe.

Through the window he saw them in their various sprawling poses as they licked their ice cream cones.

Three of them were coming across the parking lot. He noticed that their skirts were held together with a large decorative pin, so that if the pin were removed, the skirt would come undone like a bandage.

The blouse of one had come out in the back and the knee sock of another had slipped down the calf.

As they entered the Ice Cream Shoppe the tallest of them glanced past Morgan as if he were of absolutely no interest.

The sound of chattering girls rushed like heat out of the Ice Cream Shoppe in the moment the door was open.

He imagined schoolgirls did not keep themselves scrupulously clean. He thought their thighs might smell of urine.

IN THE EVENING Morgan poured himself a vodka on ice and sat in his backyard and looked at his apple tree. A light breeze blew and the apple blossoms came apart and petals spun from the tree.

Petals lay evenly in a filled circle under the tree in the dusk like a reflection of the moon on the water.

Morgan's wife had had a lovely shy smile that made her face almost pretty. She had light-green eyes which attracted him because of the traces of fear or fearful misunderstanding that registered in them like barometric events.

He heard the phone ring but when he ran inside the house he realized what he'd heard was the teary whistle of his own breath.

He put on a record of a symphony orchestra and stood on an ottoman and conducted.

He waved his arms and decided he would capture the Catholic girls' school.

He would release those in the fifth grade and under.

He would keep the others without clothes in the unfilled Olympic-sized gymnasium pool.

He would steam-heat the vast tiled structure.

The nuns would be required to apply oil to the girls' bodies.

He would keep the schoolgirls steamed and oiled.

He would give them all the right to pray, especially after one of his periodic attacks or outrages.

Morgan rose earlier than ever for his morning run. He ran through the miles of streets of his suburb, his elbows swinging in tandem from side to side, his breath like another runner behind him.

The windows of the homes were dark but lit on their faces by the amber street lamps.

The tree trunks were black, but the tree leaves were bathed on their undersides in amber light.

Everything was very still.

Rounding the corner two blocks away was a woman.

She was running toward Morgan but on the opposite side of the street.

He was astonished to see at this hour a woman in running shorts and T-shirt and Adidas shoes, with her ponytail bouncing from side to side.

She ran well.

However, her breasts were heavy for her lithe figure. They moved laggingly, as if reluctant to keep pace with the rest of her.

The woman did not acknowledge Morgan, running by him with her chin in the air, but as she passed, her left arm rose above her head and from her clenched fist she extended the middle finger.

HE DRESSED for work, made coffee, and sat in his suit and tie and watched the morning cartoons on television.

He didn't trust himself to think about his children, but he could see what they were seeing.

Drawn figures where only the mouths moved.

A kind of computerized running.

Very detailed sound explosions.

It interested him that something so untrue to life could be life.

Like Mochican head pots: Mochican pots were fashioned as human heads, and the features were painted, and the handles were the ears. The Moche had portrayed one another with these pots.

Morgan knew this in his capacity as assistant curator of pre-Columbian art at the Museum of the Under Americas in New York City.

On the four walls of his office were metal shelves stacked with head pots, items of ceramic erotica, and decorated vessels of the Mochican, Chimu, Chanca, Lupaca, and late Ancon civilizations.

Every few weeks another shipment would come in and he would fall further behind in his cataloging.

These lost peoples were obsessed with their sexual organs.

They ceramicized the organs of sex, and depicted the positions of fornication and the variations on it, including cunnilingus, sodomy, and bestiality.

Their sex organs were the biggest thing about the ancient peoples of Peru. Their legs, trunks, and heads, and thus, inescapably, their brains, were much smaller.

That is how the Incas were able to wipe them out, who were themselves not that smart, having then laid down their arms when the conquistadores came along and asked them to.

One of the captured Inca kings had offered to fill a room with gold and silver if the Spaniards would let him go. The Spaniards accepted his offer. When his subjects had filled the room with gold and silver the Spaniards thanked the king and slit his throat.

Morgan turned off the television.

He went upstairs and adjusted the shades on the bedroom windows to suggest ongoing life.

He set a clock timer in each room upstairs and down so that lamps would go on and off by themselves.

He sincerely believed that his house was not lived in and that it needed to appear otherwise to passers-by.

Through the dining-room window he saw a late-model white Cadillac pulling up at the curb in front of his house.

He stood quite still trying to think of someone he knew who drove a Cadillac.

No one got out of the car.

He ran upstairs. From his daughter's bedroom he saw, partially obscured by branches of the maple tree, a man and a woman sitting in the car.

The man was wearing a blue blazer and gray slacks. He sat with the back of his shoulder against the passenger door. His graying head of hair was well-groomed, with the tracks of the comb quite visible.

Morgan could not see the woman's face, but a slender young arm lay at rest on the steering wheel. The woman was sitting with her legs raised, and her ankles in the man's lap.

She had kicked off her shoes. Her billowy skirt had ridden up her legs.

Her stocking feet turned outward. The toes curled.

They're not people I know, Morgan thought. They have parked her Cadillac in a neighborhood where nobody knows them.

I am the lucky one chosen for my lack of consequence.

The woman clamped her knees together, then jerked them apart. She did this several times.

The man put his hand on her thigh. Then he removed his hand from her thigh and held both hands palms up, as if appealing to reason.

The woman abruptly withdrew her legs and a moment later the engine started. The man lunged forward and turned off the ignition.

Morgan went downstairs, out the rear door, which he locked after him, and he backed his own car down the driveway to the street. He wanted to see what they looked like.

The Cadillac was gone.

MORGAN HAD TRAVELED widely in the Western Hemisphere. Which country had it been where the American cultural attaché had thrown a Halloween party at his house on the bay? When Morgan had arrived by taxi the gates were blocked by mestizo men and women.

They stood in front of the cab with their hands out, they were crying in lispy Spanish, trick or treat, trick or treat, and the security guard had come out to shoo them away.

Going up the steps of the diplomatic residence, Morgan looked back and saw the mestizos with their arms waggling through the gate. They called to him with elaborate references to his noble lineage.

They were small in stature and it was impossible to tell their age. They looked as if they were made of leather.

They looked, with their dark skin and slanted cheekbones and black hair, like the sea wrack of ancient Oriental migrations.

Morgan thought of them now as he jogged in the chilly early morning after Halloween and saw relics stuck to the wet street—a child's mask, a candy wrapper, a hank of sheet imprinted with tire treads.

Coming to a corner, he turned down a winding road that he did not remember having run.

It was a steep curving downhill past stone houses set rather close considering their luxurious size.

Behind them the land angled off sharply through a stand of woods that looked over the parkway leading to the city.

He came abreast of one house of which all but the slate roof was hidden by a stone wall.

Triangles of green bottle glass were embedded in concrete along the top of the wall, and looping strands of barbed wire were fastened to steel construction rods protruding from the concrete every few yards.

The wall followed the curve of the road for some distance and at the end of it a man in a black suit was pushing open a cast-iron gate.

He was short, with skin the color of leather, and he had black hair, a prominent broken beak nose, and a narrow jaw coming to a point like an arrowhead.

The gate swung into Morgan's path and he jogged in place as a black limousine emerged from the driveway, spun sharply right with a squeal of tires, and gunned off down the hill, its brake lights flaring as it disappeared around the bend.

The limousine had been packed with men sitting shoulder to shoulder, all of them in black suits, like the gatekeeper, and all with faces of the dark mestizo aspect.

Then a station wagon emerged with a driver similarly dressed and one passenger in the back seat. She was a small mestizo girl in the Catholic girls' school uniform of maroon and white and with a stack of books in her arms.

In this way Morgan learned of the district where the houses were maintained by certain foreign governments as residences for their legations.

IN NOVEMBER, Morgan received a letter from his wife's mother. Yellow foliage filled the tree, and though the day was dark, a weird light lay over everything, as if the sun, fallen from the sky, had broken into leaves.

He drove to the diner in the old part of town in the shadow of the Thruway overpass. He took a seat at the counter and read the letter.

I know I shouldn't interfere, Morgan's wife's mother wrote, but I can't stand idly by and see my daughter suffer. Surely two reasonably intelligent people can work things out.

Morgan's wife's mother was a professor of English. By reasonably intelligent she meant two people who showed as much intelligence as could reasonably be expected of them.

Morgan's wife's family were Lutheran of German ancestry.

His family were Calvinists of French Huguenot ancestry.

The cleaning women who trudged up Morgan's street every morning from the bus stop at the bottom of the hill were Baptists of African ancestry.

The gardener who raked the leaves into a big pile in the street was Greek Orthodox of Yugoslav ancestry.

Lately, Jews of East European ancestry who had owned the dry-cleaning establishment had sold it to Buddhists of Korean ancestry.

The counterman handed him a large laminated menu and smiled a gold-toothed smile. Hey, compadre, he said.

Morgan looked at the menu: he could have the chili, or the chicken soup, he could have pigs' feet or Irish lamb stew or lasagna or souvlaki.

I am not reasonably intelligent, Morgan thought. I am unreasonably intelligent.

I suffer a vision of the incessant migrations of mankind lapping the earth prehistorically, historically, and to the present moment.

MORGAN AROSE later than usual, slipped on his sweatpants and sweatshirt, socks and running shoes, and he stepped outside.

He had slept late because a soft wet snow was falling. It had changed the sound of everything.

The snow fell soft as down on his shoulder and on his drawstring hood.

Heavy white wet snow fell past his eyes. It gathered on his eyelashes.

He ran in the middle of the street in the depression made by automobile tires.

The snow, clotting in the treads of his shoes, affected his balance and made the going difficult.

He was exhilarated by this risk of life and limb.

He came to a corner and turned down the curving hill of the foreign-legation residence because it would be more treacherous still.

A few moments later he was lifted off his feet.

He felt astounding pain in his chest. He could not breathe.

His four limbs flailing, he wheeled and tumbled helplessly through the falling snow like a swimmer inside a wave.

He found himself on his hands and knees buried in snow. A considerable time seemed to have passed.

But there was light under the snow, he could see the crystals melting before his eyes. He pawed the crystals and saw smears of red blood.

He rose, gasping for breath, snow chunks falling from him. He sank to his knees and staggered again to his feet.

The residence of the foreign legation was burning.

The legation's iron gate was torn from its hinges.

A black car door slid idly down the hill.

The falling snow was mixed with ash. Bits and pieces of metal embedded themselves in the snow around Morgan's feet.

Several schoolbooks fell from the sky.

He heard something like a flag drumming in the wind; he heard screams, shattering glass.

He picked up, and put down again, a maroon knee sock with a child's leg in it.

A woman in a running suit was coming down the hill toward him, her mouth open, her hands up at the sides of her head.

Morgan saw it was his friend who had given him that rude sign early one morning of the previous summer.

Is this something? Morgan asked her. He was embarrassed. Did I do this? he said, trying to smile, trying to make himself presentable, smoothing his hair with his bloodied hand.

THE
LEATHER
MAN

□ □ □

THEY'RE NOTHING NEW, you can read about the Leather Man, for instance, a hundred years ago making his circuit through Westchester, Connecticut, into the Berkshires in the summer, seen sitting on the roadside, glimpsed in the woods, he had these regular stops, caves, abandoned barns, riverbanks under the iron bridges in mill towns, the Leather Man, a hulk, colossally dressed, in layers of coats and shawls and pants, all topped with a stiff hand-fashioned leather outer armor, like a knight's, and a homemade pointed hat of leather, he was ten feet tall, an apparition. Of course it's the essence of these people that they're shy, they scurry at the sign of confrontation, never hurt a soul. But it was said of this fellow that when cornered he would engage in quite rational conversation, unlearned of course, with no reference to current events, and perhaps with a singular line of association that might strike one at times as not sequential, not really reasonably sequential on first audit, but genial nonetheless, with transitions made by smile or the sincere struggle for words; even the act of talking, one assumes, is something you can lose the knack of. So there is a history. And though the country of western New England or the farmlands in the north Midwest will still find one asleep in the plains, a patch of wheat flattened in his contours, say, and although they're common enough in the big cities, living in doorways, wiping your windshields with a dirty rag for a quarter, men, or carrying their bags, smoking butts from the gutters, women, or the communities of them, living each in a private alcove underground between subway stations, in the nests of the walls alongside tracks, or down under the tracks in the hollows and nooks of the electric cable conduits, what is new is the connection they're making with each other, some kind of spontaneous communication has flashed them into awareness of each other, and hell, they may as well have applied to the national endowment as a living art form, there is someone running them but I don't know who.

I don't know who and I don't know why. Conceivably it's a harmless social phenomenon, like all the other forms of suffering, that is to say not planned for a purpose but merely a natural function of everything else going, and maybe it is heartless to look askance at suffering, to be suspicious of it, Southern church blacks, welfare recipients, jobless kids around the pool halls and so on, but that's the job, that's our role, I don't think I have to justify it. We know how danger grows, or for that matter large intangible events, spiritual events, there were five six hundred thousand, yes? at that farmer's field twenty years ago, and fifty of them were us, you remember, one part per ten thousand, like the legal chemistry for a preservative, one part per ten thousand to keep the thing from turning bad. I was there myself and enjoyed the music. My favorite was Joan C. Baez, the most conservative of musicians, ultraliberal pacifist peacenik, remember peaceniks? That was a coining we did ourselves and gave it to some columnist, in Denver I think it was, spread like wildfire. But she sang nice, early in the game, everyone stoned on sun, chemical toilets still operative . . .

We found a girl there, incidentally, who was doing these strange spastic pantomimes that drew a real crowd. Beginning with her arms over her head. Brought her elbows down over the boobs, seemed to push the elbows out, pushing at something, and then one arm went around the back of the neck, and then all these gyrations of the head, it was the weirdest thing, as if she was caught in something, a web, a net, so intense, so concentrated, the crowd, the music disappeared, and then she went down on her knees and knelt through her arms like they were some kind of jump rope, and then when her arms were behind her, that was not right, she tried to get out that way, get out, she was getting out of something, enacting the attempt, face all twisted and red to get out, you see. So we took some pictures, and then we diagrammed the action and what we came up with was very interesting, it was someone in a straitjacket, it was the classic terror enacted of someone straitjacketed and trying to break free. Now, who can you think of, the person who in fact could do that, the person who could get out of straitjackets, who was that? he said.

Houdini.

That's right, Houdini, it was one of his routines, getting out of the kind of straitjacket to break the heart.

TO DO HERMITAGE, the preference for one's own company. Picture yourself in such solitude, in natural surroundings, say, the classical version. Build a hut in the woods, split your own logs, grow things, ritualize daily subsistence, listen to the wind sing, watch the treetops dance, feel the weather, feel yourself in touch with the way things are. You remember your Thoreau. There's a definite political component to avoiding all other human beings and taking on the coloration of your surroundings, invisible as the toad on the log. Whatever the spiritual content, it is the action of hiding out, you see these guys hide out. So the question is, why? It may be a normal life directed by powerful paranoidal impulses, or it may be a paranoid life that makes sense given the particular individual's background. But something has happened. If he is hiding, I want to know why.

But supposing on the other hand we all seek to impose the order we can manage, the more public the order the better we are known. Politicians are known. Artists are known. They impose public order. But say you are some hapless fellow, you can't keep a job, the wife nags, the children are vicious, the neighbors snigger. Down in your basement, though, you make nice things of wood. You make a bookshelf, you make a cabinet, sawing and planing, sanding, fitting, gluing, and you construct something very fine, you impose that order, that is the realm of your control. You make a bigger cabinet. You make a cabinet you can walk into. You build it where nobody will watch you. When it is done, you walk inside and lock the door.

BEFORE WE BREAK for lunch, let me propose this idea. You have them walking into their boxes and locking the door behind them. Fine. But two people do that and you have a community. You see what I'm saying? You can make a revolution with people who have nothing to do with each other at the same time. There is a theory, for instance, that the universe oscillates. It is not a steady beaming thing, nor did it start with a bang. It expands and contracts, inhales and exhales, it is either growing larger than you can imagine or imploding toward a point. The crucial thing is its direction. If things come apart enough, they will have started to come together.

0001. MEMBERS OF THE CLASS: feral children, hermits, street people, gamblers, prisoners, missing persons, forest-fire wardens, freaks, permanent invalids, recluses, autistics, road tramps, the sensory deprived. (See also astronauts.)

WE BORROWED an ordinary precinct car and went looking for one. Contact on Fourteenth Street and Avenue A, time of contact ten-thirteen P.M. Subject going east on southside Fourteenth Street.

White, female, indeterminate age. Wearing WWII-issue khaki great-coat over several dresses, gray fedora over blue watch cap, several shawls, some kind of furred shoes overlaid with galoshes. Stockings rolled to ankles over stockings. Pushing two-wheeled grocery cart stuffed with bags, sacks, rags, soft goods, broken umbrellas. Purposeful movements. Subject went directly from public trash receptacles to private trash deposits in doorways, seemed interested in anything made of cloth. Subject sat down to rest, back to fence, East Fifteenth Street. This is the site of Consolidated Edison generating plant. Subject slept several hours on sidewalk in twenty-degree weather. At four A.M. awakened by white male derelict urinating on her.

BANCROFT SUGGESTS as an organizing principle we make the distinction between simple and profound dereliction. Ignore bums in the pokey and the poor slobs who shoot up. Always the snob, Bancroft. He wants only middle-class-and-above material? Still, there's something to be said: If the brain is overrun, where is the act of separation? If nothing is excluded, the meaning is lost. Interesting he designates as profound that which is incomplete.

IN THE CITY of New Rochelle, N.Y., a man was apprehended as a Peeping Tom. He'd been found in the landscaping behind the residence of Mr. and Mrs. Morris Wakefield, 19 Croft Terrace. He had the aspect of a wild man, bearded, unkempt, ragged. Reported to have been glimpsed several times over a period of months in backyards of the better neighborhoods of the city. No identification.

Slater sat up and took notice. The incident had so shocked Mrs. Morris Wakefield that she had been placed under sedation. Poor woman was in no shape. Already under severe stress as a result of the disappearance of her husband, Morris Wakefield, a partner in a bridge-construction firm, an engineer of considerable reputation in his field, no known enemies. Exemplary life. Gone. The couple was childless. They had been married twelve years. We went up there. Alone and grieving in her home, Mrs. Wakefield had prepared for bed and came downstairs in her negligee for a glass of warm milk. Two eerie eyes rolled along the rim of the windowsill. She screamed and ran upstairs and locked herself in her bedroom, where she phoned the police. I find, not infrequently, quote New Rochelle police detective Leo Kreisler, trouble breaks out in a rash, we have people in our community we have no dealings with for twenty years, and suddenly everything goes at once, someone is robbed, then hurt in a car a week later, or someone is beat up and a relative steals money, and just like that one family is in multiple crisis in the space of a few days. We asked to see him. Sure, why not, quote Detective Kreisler. Who knows, maybe he'll like you. He doesn't talk, he doesn't eat, he looks at you like he's thinking of something else.

The prisoner wore floppy chino slacks torn down one leg and belted with a piece of clothesline, dirty white Stan Smith tennis sneakers, no socks, a stained and greasy workshirt. He was not a trim person, but a person who looked formerly fat. Pants and shirt hung on him. Badly needed a haircut, and in the fluorescent light of the slammer blinked with the weak eyes and pale doughy undereyes of a person who wears glasses without his glasses. His beard white, although his matted hair reddish. He sat cross-legged on the vinyl floor. He sat with the fingers of his hands intertwined stiffly. Slater contemplated him. He was all connected, his legs crossed, his fingers laced. Under observation he raised his knees still crossed and roped, his wrists around them, his fingers still locked.

Slater: Are you in fact the owner of the property on which you were apprehended, the bridge engineer Morris Wakefield, the missing husband?

The peeper nodded yes.

AN ITEM from the files of the security department of National Dry Foods Corporation: One of their young marketing executives had been relocated from Short Hills, New Jersey, to Flint, Michigan. It was discovered sometime thereafter that in Flint he was living in domicile with a woman not his wife and two children not his children, although he represented them as such. Six months it took them to find his legal wife and two children: They were still in place in their Short Hills, New Jersey, home, living in domicile with an executive of the company who had been relocated from Flint. The two executives had been fraternity brothers at Duke University.

SLATER, do you fuck around?

A long time before answering. No.

So do I. Let me tell you about the lunch I had yesterday. A very beautiful lady whom I've had my eye on for years. She and my wife are pals, they go to the galleries together. Well, we were all at this party and I make a joke, a signal joke, clearly funny if she doesn't pick up on it but a signal in case she wants to. Is that how you do it?

No, I usually come right out with it.

Well, I'm older than you are. I'm a different generation. Wit counts for me, the double entendre. So we had lunch. I could hardly hold her down. She was ready to avenge fifteen years of faithful marriage. Not only that her husband cheated on her, but that he was nasty at home. Not only that he was nasty and mean, but that he had no respect for what she did and made fun of the causes she supported. Not only that he lacked respect, but that he was infantile and went all to pieces when he cut himself shaving. And not only that, but that he spent no time with the children and complained when he had to shell out money for their school.

Slater smiled.

Oh God, it was uncanny. Like she had held up a mirror. I found myself getting defensive, wanting to argue. It finally comes down to a smile, a small kindness, a bit of good cheer, she said. Those are the important things. Your husband is a cheerful man, I said, and by this time in the conversation I didn't want to have anything more to do with her. An amiable, charming man, I said, with a good sense of humor. Oh yes, she said, so was Dr. Jekyll.

What is the essential act of the Leather Man? He makes the world foreign. He distances it. He is estranged. Our perceptions are sharpest when we're estranged. We can see the shape of things. Do you accept this as a principle? All right, then, consider something as common as philandering. I'm an old-fashioned fellow and I use old-fashioned words. After a while your marriage becomes your cover. Don't laugh, I'm quite serious. Your feelings are broken down by plurality, you don't stop, you keep moving, it becomes your true life to keep moving, to keep moving emotionally, you find finally the emotion in the movement. You are the Leather Man, totally estranged from your society, the prettiest women are rocks in the stream, flowers along the road, you have subverted your own life and live alone in the wild, your only companion your thoughts.

I think what I'm proposing is a structure, not a theory of a subversive class, but an infrastructure of layered subversion, perhaps not conspiracy at all. That something has happened like a rearrangement of molecules, and that since we are political persons here we are sensitive to the crude politics of it, we think of it as some sort of ground for antisocial action when it might not be that at all. So I'm saying the way to understand it for our particular purposes might be not the usual thing of getting inside, penetration, but distance, putting it away from us, getting as far from it as possible, to see what it really is. Because if it has gotten outside us, and we're inside and we can't see the shape of it, it comes to us as reality and it has no meaning at all.

W E ' V E   G O T   this astronaut who went bad, James C. Montgomery, who took a hero's welcome in 1966 and since then has been picked up for stock fraud, embezzlement, forgery, drunken driving —you name it, he's done it: stealing cars, assault, assault with a deadly weapon. This sometimes happens to individuals in whom history intensifies like electroshock, leaves them all scattered afterward. We've got him quiet now, but his wife keeps talking to reporters down in Florida and threatens suit.

I'll read you part of the interrogation by one of the staff psychiatrists:

Were you ever frightened? Did anything happen on the mission you didn't report?

No sir.

Did anything unexpected happen?

No sir.

Did the idea of space hold any terror for you? Being out there so far from home?

Question repeated.

No, well, you do your job, you're busy as hell, there's no time to think, and you're always in touch, almost always in touch, control voice in the empyrean void. No, I would say not. *(pause)* You just keep your nose to the panel. Make community with the switches, little lights. Everything around you is manmade, you have that assurance. *(pause)* American-made.

But then you did the landing, right?

Yes sir.

You walked.

Yes sir.

You got out of the machine and walked around.

Yes sir. Oh—for a while there I was alone and miserable inside my space suit. Is that what you mean?

I have the feeling you're trying to tell me what you think I want to hear.

Well, shit. *(pause)* Look, the truth is I don't remember. I mean, I remember that I walked on the moon but now I can see it on television and I don't feel it, you know what I mean? I can't believe it happened. I see myself, that I did it, but I don't remember how it felt, I don't remember the experience of it.

CAN I JUST TRY a quick simple experiment here? Five minutes of your time? Silence. Slater looked around the table. Someone lit a pipe. The grudging tribal assent. I'm going to give you a list of simple nouns and ask you to respond—just fill me in on what's happening. All right?

Night. Ladder. Window. Scream. Penis.

Have you been talking to my wife? someone said. Everyone laughed.

Patrol. Mud. Flare. Mortar.

All right, someone said.

President. Crowd. Bullet. Slater said, We've got thousands of people in this country whose vocation it is to let us know what our experience is. Are you telling me this is not a resource?

Slate, we're going to have a fight on our hands if you want to admit that kind of material. You don't know the minds you're dealing with. They're not going to understand, they're going to read it as source. Then you know how messy it'll get? You're going to have to interrogate these resources, the most articulate people in the land, the ones who already have their hackles up, and you're going to ask them where they got their information?

No, you're not hearing me, Slater said. We'll know where they got their information. We gave it to them.

LIVES
OF THE
POETS

□   □   □

MY LEFT THUMB is stiff, not particularly swollen although the veins at the base are prominent and I can't move it backward or pick up something without pain. Have I had this before? It's vaguely familiar to me and it may subside, but it feels, bulging veins and all, as if it won't, it is either gout or arthritis unless, of course, death to the writer, it is that monstrous Lou Gehrig thing, God save us all.

Also I have a touch of pinched nerve in the neck. Does this relate to the thumb? What is happening here? I'm a true Capricorn, my destiny is to grind to death.

And then of course this subtle hearing impairment. Every once in a while I hear the voice but not the words. Is the cervical pinch constricting sound, pinching me into silence? What can I do about this? Why don't I go to a doctor? Oh creeping ruin! Like that caved-in tenement I saw on East Sixth Street, the sky showing through the roof, whole trees growing up through the floors, weeds sprouting, vines cascading from the windows—a Manhattan Congo, an upriver interior of toucan-spattered darkness. Monkey screech, ohdee death! And in the moonoil murk of the basement a flatheaded croc eying me.

Where is that nimbleness I never had? Where is that mind and body harmonic, that dream life in which I thoughtfully chew my food and take little sips of spring water, and I move in the philosophically enlightened way, and I breathe from the diaphragm, a totally realized being in a serenity of pacific emotion, unself-censorious, without guilt, without shame, fulfilled in each moment of life and memory and loving anticipation as the leanest brownberry guru? I can't even stand up straight without wincing.

I don't smoke anymore, that's something, I've cut down on beer and know clean air when I smell it, I know to eat bran, and acerola rose hips, and that sugar is bad and salt is bad and eggs and anything pickled, smoked, or cured. But it's too much—all over the city everyone running shopping consulting, trying to get away from this white-bread life, in their running suits they run, with their vegetable juicers under their arms, I've got more important things to do. What I need is a master guide to the wisdom, an exclusive service in the ideal location of the world, say, where you give all your money and all you ever hope to have, and in return you receive a generosity of beneficent hygienically balanced natural unradiated lifelight and you get to live and write a minimum hundred and fifty years, give or take a decade, and the cock never fails you.

Which brings me to our major occupation.

The other night Brad walked into Elio's with his friend and there was his wife, Moira, having dinner with her Women's Political Caucus. Guess what happened to me? Brad said on the phone the next day. Your wife saw you at dinner with your friend, I said, because Angel, my wife, had already told me the story because Moira had confided it to her. I felt so humiliated, Moira told Angel. After all, I know the whole town knows about Brad's affairs, he makes no effort to hide them. But this time here I am expounding to my colleagues on the specifically feminist thing and in walks my husband with this dollie on his arm.

What did you have? I said to Brad. The house pasta and a zinfandel, he said. I was expecting the end when I got home, but all Moira said was, Brad, I'm not giving up on this marriage, it's been too good. He laughed wryly. Brad goes all over the world for his column and when he's home he spends his time playing tennis. In fact, that's how he met this lady.

Brad's friend is not a dollie, I made the mistake of saying to Angel. She's a jock. Oh, said Angel. What does she look like? I only saw her from the next court, I said. Comic-book pretty. The spunky-heroine type. And lo, Angel's flinty look came upon her: You might be describing Moira, she said. That's what always happens—they go for someone who looks like the wife.

Angel is gathering tales of male perfidy: Up in New Haven after Ralph broke up with *his* young woman, he had the insensitivity to bring home to Rachel the colored briefs he had acquired. I refuse anymore your underwear to wash, said Rachel, who's Hungarian. Red was the color the girl had chosen for her professor poet, in some unfortunate and unnecessarily symbolic way the color had run in the washing machine and red dye got over all Rachel's sheets, towels, and so forth. Ralph also brought home some records the girl gave him and when he listens to them Rachel runs upstairs and shuts her door, the music staining her brain as the dye did her lingerie.

Why are men so awful? Angel said. I agree. Ralph is disgustingly truthful, he has this rage to confess. He told Rachel of his affair almost from the moment of its inception. Of course, she found it far worse than his actually going out and fucking someone that he wanted to discuss it with her, as if he needed her approval in some odd, unhinged way.

But everyone talks too much—Rachel broadcasting all of this— the women, the wives, talk constantly and tell things to each other you'd think they'd have the sense to keep to themselves. They violate their own privacy and everything gets hung on the line as if we all live in some sort of marital tenement. Whatever happened to discretion? Where is pride? What has caused this decline in tact and duplicity?

And then of course I suffer for it. A couple we know will split and I am told by my wife what yet another defective man has done to the perfectly fine woman who had the bad sense years before to marry him. You look at any couple we know, Angel says. The woman is better put together, she has read more, she is more intelligent and far kinder than the man. We go to a dinner party and the woman's conversation is far more interesting.

I notice this bump on my ankle seems to be getting bigger. The hell. And my throat is scratchy this morning. I just got over laryngitis, what is happening to me?

On the other hand, this is the Village, whatever can be tried to stem disaster is tried here, so I'm ready for action. A free paper found in the lobby tells all about it: I can begin with lessons in the Alexander technique, a proven method for attaining awareness and physical reeducation and postural alignment, and then I can go buy the Bach Flower Remedies, look in on the Breathing Center, stop awhile at the Center for Jewish Meditation and Healing, sign up for some t'ai chi exercise in flowing motion for vitality and health, and if things still don't work out, I can submit myself to some deep-tissue manipulation by a qualified Rolfer. The Gurdjieff discussion group might come in handy, and if I need some companionship the Loving Brotherhood is there making "the planet a place where it is safe for people to love each other." Can't knock that. When I get some pots and pans I can do a little gourmet vegetarian cooking and, restored in my energy balance, go out then for a whack at some Functional Integration with the Feldenkrais Method. The Vedanta Society will bring all these things together for me, or else I can drop in to the local Tranquility Tank, where I can float in a body-temperature solution free from gravity. I feel better already.

But as I make my way along these various paths to fulfillment, maybe I ought to take some martial-arts training so I can kick the shit out of anyone who tries to stop me.

Another couple we are all watching are Llewellyn and Anne. Llewellyn has gone on a Zen retreat in Vermont that will last three months. When he gets home he'll let his hair grow back in and then sometime next year he'll shave his head again and go away for four months or five months, he is serious about this and so there's no telling where this will lead, eventually they turn celibate, don't they? And where will that leave Anne? Right now she has to drive to Vermont to see her husband. Llewellyn has been doing Zen for years and in fact has attained the rank of monk. That is something less than a *sensei* but it is serious stuff. This last time he left, Anne threw a party for him and she held up, all right, she was cheerful and steadfast, and we all drank and ate and laughed and had a good time, but Llewellyn was in a lousy mood. I felt he resented it that we weren't trying to discourage him from going, so as to make him feel more heroic about the whole thing. But why do that? He'd shaved his head after all, poor prickly Llewellyn. He looks very good in his ascetic mode, he's about five eight with a firm round belly, when he removes his horn-rims you see what might be Oriental facial planes, a saffron complexion; the more he has studied, the more his appearance has changed. I fully believe in his capacities as a Zen monk, I'm willing to forgive him anything because he's a good poet. Also I like it that Zen monks are self-centered, snobbish, moody, that they blame their wives when things go wrong, grouse at their children and hate like hell to lose at games. Makes me feel I have a shot at being a Zen monk too someday.

But I'm talking about couples no longer entirely together, I'm talking about *the infinite task of the human heart.* That's a Delmore Schwartz line. In the war between Angel and me we have reached the stage where we send in other marriages to do the fighting.

Llewellyn is my heavy gun, he suggests some mysterious need not susceptible to clinical analysis, some wild dignity given to men our age that the behaviorists can't account for. He sits up in some drafty farmhouse with his legs crossed twenty hours a day, I mean they really meditate in those Zen retreats, there is absolutely no fucking around. And all Angel has been able to muster by way of defense is to say that she's always detected a selfishness in the Zen Buddhist idea, but there is probably an answer to this if I know my Zen which I don't which means I do.

Oh oh, there's another one, they make these forays, you can see they're game, it's not their fault that they crawl and are loathsome. I find if I sprinkle boric acid on them they're easier to see, they plod right on like arctic explorers. Why do we revile them so? This fellow is nine stories over the street, he is colonizing an award-winning high-rise, he wants to bring roach civilization to the wilderness of strange hard highly lit surfaces, a mineral terrain, like the moon, where nothing grows. The other day I slapped the kitchen counter behind one of them to see what he would do and he didn't scurry off down the side of the counter, he leapt into the canyon between the counter and the refrigerator, they do what they have to, like Butch Cassidy and the Sundance Kid, they surprise you, they surprise themselves, they're unpredictable under stress, like us, maybe that's why we revile them.

Actually I think they are what keep Angel from following me here. She's afraid when I come home that I bring them with me in my luggage. When she comes to town and joins me for a drink she looks at the walls the ceiling the floor before she sits down. Maybe the more she sees of them the more accustomed she'll become. Except I can't believe that, Angel is the Princess Fastidious, the cleanest person in the world, when she is not doing anything she is cleaning tidying ordering throwing out, not even Nature is immune to her ruthless tidying, she will weed, prune, clip, she likes to cut off things that stick out, as I've told her many times, but in the house, her home, the cosmos is tidied before the disorder can even think of occurring, I've had to clutch at half-finished cups of coffee flying off the table, grab my dinner plate, pluck open unopened mail from the trash, clasp the morning newspaper to my bosom, lash myself to the newel post to withstand her gale wind of tidiness. Is it me she's trying to blow away? One day last week she called, her voice happy, she was in a really good mood, the contractor had just finished installing the new septic tank. I wanted to share her joy. I said why not have a big party where everybody goes to the bathroom.

They have taken all morning to erect a scaffold in front of the United Thread Mills sign. From this distance they look like painters with their white caps, but they are hammering things into the building brick.

Last night Paul gave a birthday dinner for Brigitte, whom he loves but is slow to marry. Paul writes screenplays and loves Brigitte in part because she is not an actress, has no interest in the theater, and does not wish to write or direct films. He booked Texarkana because she's from New Orleans. Brigitte is green-eyed and red-haired and used to hang out with the Democratic political crowd down there. Not much left to learn after a barbecue like that. She had a joke for us: *Why do women have cunts?* We waited. *So that men will talk to them.* Angel likes Brigitte a lot. We were three couples at the table, the third being Freddy and Pia. Freddy spends his days now trying to live down his Pulitzer in fiction. He adores Pia, who is a tiny beauty with a bright mind and a lovely laugh, and has a good job in advertising, but he is as slow to marry her as Paul is to marry Brigitte. Nevertheless both relationships seem to be secure, as I notice is the case when there is at least a twenty-year difference in ages between the man and the woman. Sometimes Freddy and Pia go out together with Freddy's daughter by an early marriage, Kimberly. Pia and Kimberly really get along, as why not, since they are the same generation.

The most erotic dance I ever saw: a father and his daughter waltzing at a bar mitzvah at the Fifth Avenue Hotel. I've never seen ecstasy to match that, the slight thin girl in her black velvet jumper and white hose leaning her back into the hand of her handsome father as he twirled her about and they stared into each other's eyes.

Sometimes I look at myself, Freddy once said, and I think I've got a big one. Other times, I don't know, it looks small to me.

Brad once told me he did not take baths because he does not like to look at his body.

On the other hand, my friend Sascha bathes for hours, he writes his stories on a reading board that rests on the sides of the tub, and reads his students' stories, and in fact conducts his entire intellectual life in water.

Sam told me he jumps into the lake behind his house after a sauna even in winter. That's what makes movie stars. Sam, the best-looking, most famous actor in the world, once said to Freddy: I'm lonely, you know any girls?

I am not talking about divorced couples, you understand, but couples not entirely together. Let's make some useful distinctions here. On the one side are the traditionally married, battling, shrieking, and occupying each other's brains like some terrible tumor until one of them dies. My parents had a classic textbook marriage like that . . . On the other are those marriages that need to be severed instantly, after a few months, days, hours, marriages so clearly disastrous, unconsummatable, perhaps, that even the lawyers moving in to mop up forbear the long faces and dispatch the thing as efficiently as possible.

Swinging pendulously between these two archetypes, touching on both but wanting to be neither, are the marriages of my generation.

I see what they're doing, they're attaching the scaffold to the brick siding, story by story, putting the thing up as they go. They were at Thread Mills yesterday, today they're six feet above at United. Like rock climbers, faces against the siding, they hammer away, four stories over West Houston Street. It's peculiar that through all the rumbling truck traffic, sirens, horns, I can hear clearly up here the piccolo taps of their hammers.

And down below them, curling around the corner from Greene Street, little kids strung out behind the teacher's outstretched arms, hand in tiny hand, fluttering and waving like patchwork pennants. She strains and leans forward, pulling them like an old monoplane dragging an advertisement through the sky.

So we have the phenomenon of the neither married nor divorced but no longer entirely together. There is a moving of husbands into their own digs, their own long days and nights. There is a casting off of establishment. How does it begin? After you're married for several years you start waiting, and you don't even realize it, you become alert to something at the edge of the forest, you look up from your grazing and it isn't even there, the delicate sense behind all events all occasions of putting in time, marking time, killing time. Isn't that so, compadre? I mean bear with me even though you think I'm taking strength from numbers: You notice younger men than you going off stunningly from coronaries, embolisms, aneurysms, sudden cancerous devastations, every manner of swift scything, the achievement of their lives still to come. From one moment to the next, all that feisty character is plaintive, all that intention and high design has turned to pathos, and the custom-tailored suits are specters in the closet. And what they did, these raucous, smartass go-getters, turns out to be shamefully modest, of little consequence, they were their own greatest publicists and all the shouting was their own. So my discovery at fifty is that this mortal rush to solitude is pandemic, that is the news I bring. It is not that everyone I know is fucked up, incomplete, unrealized. On the whole we are all quite game. It's life itself that seems to be wanting.

After all, as I told my friend Sascha, who came over to have a drink and look around, I've achieved a body of work and recognition for it, I have money enough, I've got four children, whom I love and whom I hope soon to raise to reasonable levels of self-sufficiency. My wife is quick-witted and attractive. We own a house with a mortgage in the forest and a house with a mortgage at the seashore, I have reasonable opportunities to travel wherever I wish, and, insofar as Angel's worst suspicions can be realized in this studio I've set up for myself in bohemia, I'm fairly sure I can summon any one of a half-dozen women who on little or no notice will be delighted to spend the night with me. That's a modest estimate. They will get in their cars, fly in from other cities. Yet I call no one, I isolate myself, a man whose state of rest is inconsolability. I walk the streets feeling like a vagrant, I've got this stinging desolation in my eyes.

I've got this painful stitch in the kidney.

Jesus Christ, after a while you know you just don't look up in New York when you hear the sirens. There was just a full-complement arrest right out the window nine stories down on Houston, three cop cars parked askew, couple of blue-and-white motor scooters, a dozen cops and plainclothesmen milling about at the Mobil gas station and one slender man, hands cuffed behind his back, being shoved into an unmarked car with a turning red light on the roof. And sitting with the last paragraph, I missed the whole thing.

Of course, this entire neighborhood brims with aspiration. Winos come into the street with their incredibly filthy greasy rags and wipe at the windshields of the cars waiting at the traffic lights and then they hold their hands out for the tip. They're never threatening, they can be turned away except you won't know that if you have a Jersey plate. They will go back to the sidewalk and smoke and strut and laugh till the next light. When it's cold they'll build a fire in an oil drum.

Downstairs Jake the doorman has his eye open for the main chance. He's rooted in his place, what chance does he have? But he's made of himself an entrepreneur, people come past him in and out every day in this high-rise, must be six hundred people living in this building. Jake smiles, delivers messages, holds packages, helps with bags, watches cars, children, accepts gratuities. He's also the agent for cleaning women, window washers, car services, exterminators. Your doorman Jake is a good man, he says, but a poor man. Can he simonize your car? Can he chauffeur for you? You need your floors buffed, he will go out and rent a machine and take care of it after his shift. You need furniture moved, he'll go out and find a truck somewhere. Fix your toaster. Paint your walls, he's the universal job service, doorman division.

Your doorman Jake is a good man but a poor man. I have an alpaca coat. He eyes me one cold day. When you finish with it, he says, remember me. That's the coat I want. A roguish smile, big teeth, he likes style, handsome black man with mustache. He has also admired my hat.

It would be terrifically convenient if things were great between my wife and me. Everything is in place, after all. She tells me we've done the hard stuff, the years that are left should be the good ones. So they should. I try to imagine the state of serene contentment in love, the coincidence of affections, a guileless generosity of soft lips, laughter and lust, and joy in the new day. Your dream is a warning, the frau doctor tells me. She is not terribly impressed by my theory of the slack marriage. You're reaching the point at which either decision would be better than what you are doing to yourself now.

Which is what my friend Sascha said when he looked around this half-furnished space. Either move in or move out is what Sascha said.

So the other evening I meet Angel and we go to the Women's Political Caucus benefit about which Moira had been having dinner with her colleagues that night Brad her husband walked in with his girlfriend. The benefit is held in this luxurious apartment on Beekman Place and consists of everyone standing around in the library getting a winebreath and then gathering in the living room for a program of songs by several women singers from Broadway shows each coming up and doing a turn with a piano accompaniment on the theme of women—how they are strong and steadfast and wonderful and can take anything but, on the other hand, how they should not be afraid to try their wings or dare to be butterflies and let their souls fly. Just before the singing starts I see Brad place his glass of wine carefully on an art-deco side table of burled wood and disappear in the direction of the front door. I by stupid comparison have been caught in the crush along the back wall behind rows of filled bridge chairs, no way I cannot hear the entire program. The pianist sets the tone with those lyrical arpeggios, those splashy chords and dramatic bass octaves of showbiz, and here is Feminism in the voice of detestable Broadway culture, her mouth open, her arms embracing air, her lepidopterous palms folding and unfolding, and a woman photographer jumping on a chair to shoot the action. But the last number is a good one, a classy little singer comes on and she's got real style, she's very modish in one of those crumpled tailored suits with an open-necked silk blouse, and standing with her hands in her jacket pockets she sings in French an American pop song with the passionate truculence of a Piaf, and then takes her hands out of her pockets and spits out the lyrics in English, that song the women love, she's telling this man who's returned who needs you who wants you, I'll survive, I'll survive, and she really raises the temperature of the place, cries of excitement, little gurgles all over the room as she tells the man in the song to get out, that she doesn't want him back, that he's not welcome anymore, that she will survive without him. And the house comes down as she walks off throwing away a curtain line all her own, not in the song—hey, wait, where are you going?

Where I'm going is down to the mailbox to see if I've heard from the Dark Lady of my sonnets.

Well, there's always tomorrow. I console myself with the year-end appeals for tax-deductible contributions: Save the Whales, Save the Seal Pups, Save the Brazilian Jungle. The Brazilian jungle? See, we're losing millions of square miles of it a year: The Brazilian jungle goes, and the whole planet's ecosystem goes with it, the bottom drops out of the weather and we're into another ice age. Christ, I didn't think I'd have to worry about the Brazilian jungle. Save the Children, Save Your Alma Mater, send to the father who runs that Times Square shelter for the runaway kid hustlers, save the Bill of Rights, get rid of handguns, stop prayer in schools, save the Native Americans, save the blacks, save us from ourselves, *Dios mío,* save us from drink and herpes, save us from pissing in space, and from our smiling elected image, and from solemn Chernenko, and save us dear God from their thundersticks.

Most of this stuff isn't even addressed to me, it's to the occupant of 9E. Well, it's nice to be welcome in the neighborhood. I see where members of a Chinese youth gang are the suspects in the murder of Kai-fan Cheng, age fourteen, they crashed a party for Oriental high-school students the other night. The Dancing Demons is the name of the gang, but there's never just one gang, their archenemies are the Wind Phantoms. The Phantoms do the protection thing, bounce for the illegal gambling joints, deal maybe. The Demons run the same shit one block over. Every once in a while there's a tong war and everyone's income drops.

I am one of the few people of my acquaintance who know that

an immigrant Chinese botanist from Szechuan province in 1926 crossed a Chinese orange with a Belgian orange and so invented the American citrus industry.

I see Chinese kids peddling Maoist tabloids at the Astor Place subway station. Mostly girls. They've got this little party going. All sorts of Chinese things going on.

When I ride the subway now I feel the real trip is down the steps, somewhere along the line everyone I knew got off and started taking taxis. I'm back in the immigrated universe, I see the phone-company ad telling us there's now an edition of the Yellow Pages in Spanish, that's interesting, and I see the shadow paintings on the station platforms, that's interesting. And now I have with one glance solved a mystery, I will eventually provide explanations of all the Mysteries, the lines at Nazca, the stone heads of Easter Island, Stonehenge, vessels that sail with no crew, and so on, but now I'll explain graffiti. Graffiti is the longing of the soot-choked urban heart for the sun life of the tropics. Tell the mayor if he'll paint the subway cars in profusions of tropical colors no one'll lay a spray can on them. And the earphones, that's interesting. I do a survey in the car, one two three four sets of earphones hooked to the little tape players, and here's something out of the quaint past, a man reading a book. When I rode the subways as a kid, I read books from the public library, I read big fat *Les Misérables* for weeks while I took the IRT to the doctor for my Wednesday allergy shots, I needed to know Jean Valjean lived a more miserable life than I did. But listening to music in the dragon's throat? Who are these people listening their way back from literacy? Before we learned to write, the world worked in a different system of perception, voices were disembodied, tales were told, ghosts spoke through shamans, we were brother to the animals, am I right? God stopped talking to humans only when they wrote about it in the Bible. On the other hand, what's different after all: you give the people little earphones, they put them on, show them a screen, they watch it, recite a spell, they go under, sing, they sing along. Hems go up go down, for a while all these idiots in bars wore cowboy hats, me I've never found a hat that looks right on me, never found a style of hat I felt right in, real in, fedora, homburg, Swiss Tirol, Irish tinker, deerhound, Russian lamb, baseball, ten-gallon, seaman watch, Greek fisher, garrison, pith or steel helmet, on me they're all dunce caps. Not just hats but all clothes, nothing ever fits right or is quite perfect, or buttons properly or has no crease across the shoulder blades or goes with a tie or without a tie, my neck is too thick for turtlenecks, my eyes too close together for aviator glasses, if I have the right shirt the trousers are in the cleaner's, I can't wear vests running shorts chains medallions watches rings cravats black ties. I feel OK only in old sweaters and corduroys and scuffed ankle boots, no pretension there, my Einstein look, no threat there, world, amiable me—slightly distracted, absent-minded, sans sexual provocation—I lose change and misplace keys, I smile boyishly, invite proprietary attention from women, I am fond and gentle, my curious mind uncontaminated by rage.

The word on Jeanie and Nick is that they are OK, they are working things out, and I am glad for that, but Nick has done something odd, he is just fifty, and he has dug an enormous hole in his basement. They live in a town house in Philadelphia, four stories of totally planned tastefully designed luxury, and the top floor is completely given over to Nick's studio, complete with word processor, Tunturi exercycle, and Everlast punching bag. Jeanie, who produces local TV news, is gone all day, their kid leaves early in the morning for Foxglove or wherever it is, but showing me around the other day, Nick said he felt impinged on, crowded, Jeanie was moving in too close, buying him things, surprises, track lighting for his office, the unabridged seventeen-volume *OED*, he was choking to death. And so, he said, leading me down to the basement and then another flight below that, he'd hired a contractor, and a half-dozen men with shovels had hand-dug the cold packed colonial dirt under the house and here in this subbasement they had built a study for him where there was no phone, it was totally soundproof and nobody was allowed in, not his kid not his wife. He opened a padlocked door with a key, turned on a light and ushered me in: Nick, it's terrific, I said as he gazed at me in fierce triumph, really great, I said, standing in this chill catacomb admiring the beads of sweat on the wood paneling. For a present I'm sending him a cask of Amontillado.

The bell.

My bookcases have arrived, this is a very sacred joy.

Goddammit, they were unassembled. I consign to the nethermost shit-filled pits of hell the misanthrope who invented Do-It-Yourself. May he do it to himself till the end of time, I've got a bashed thumb, metal splinters in the soft flesh of my hands. Made in Yugoslavia ... My friend Tasich is from Dubrovnik, I see him I'm going to kick his ass.

And here it is, the worst of hours, as drink in hand for my few days of freedom I stupidly make the call I shouldn't make. She has her drink in hand too, I can tell. How are things at the seraglio? she says. Come on, Angel, don't start. The other night at David and Nora's I was really hurt when you told everyone I had visitation rights. It was a joke! Nobody laughed. I work here, Angel, it's my retreat, like Llewellyn's ashram or whatever the hell he calls it. It sounds fine when you explain it, Jonathan. But when I try to explain it people look at me as if I'm incredibly stupid. Families of inmates in prison have visitation rights, I say. I was suggesting writing is like a sentence—it's a prison image. It's an exclusionary image as far as I'm concerned. You've locked me out. Angel, we talked about this. I construe my having the only key as a sense of sole possession, a territory of my own, a place where I can be by myself and work. It's not that I want to walk in on you, Jonathan. I don't know what's real when I'm not trusted by my own husband. There is a pause. I also think it's bad that you're the only one to have a key—it's not safe. What do you think might happen? I said. I don't know. What if you become ill? What if you're incapacitated? What if you break your leg, have a heart attack, come down with a stroke? That's very considerate of you, Angel.

Christ, she's already staked out this place with her underwear which she left drying on the shower bar and her bathrobe hanging in the closet and her contact-lens lotion in the medicine cabinet. What does she want! Wherever I go she has to go. Sometimes we go out, she'll dress in the colors I have on. She affects mannish style, linen jackets and slacks in the summer, a tie loosely knotted at the collar. It's hard to see what's happening because all of them are in drag this year. I only resent it on her. Sometimes when she talks seriously, thoughtfully she rubs her chin as I rub mine.

I see what they're doing now, they're breaking through the brick, making a window. They've knocked out half the U, the left edge of the N, they're destroying United Thread Mills, how do you like that, these guys are tottering on a scaffold four stories up, risking their skulls so some invert can have light in his loft. They won't be able to get down except by knocking out the brick and going in. It's cold too, the mast on the World Trade Center frozen to the sky.

So I pull jury duty. I am empaneled for a suit brought by a young woman against the conglomerate owners of a string of resort hotels specializing in singles-fun management. The young woman, Deirdre X, went by herself to one of these hotels in the Caribbean, named Captain Kiss's Island or something equally appalling, where, as advertised, the hotel staff took steps to maximize her social opportunities. One day, for instance, she and several guests were bused to a lovely and remote beach and there plied with rum and wine punch and set about various fun games and exercises. Eventually they were advised that these games and exercises were best done in the buff. Deirdre X deposes that she shed her inhibitions and leaped about bare-assed in the sun. She found herself attracted to a particular bare-assed young man. Others were pairing off and disappearing behind the dunes and so did they, gigglingly, hie themselves to a quiet glade in the tall beach grass. The wind whispering gently, the blue Caribbean rollers washing the shore, Deirdre X engaged in oral sex upon the young man. This was narrated as delicately as possible in high-tech Latin by her lawyer, a Bobby Kennedy look-alike who wore a brown suit with a vest. The panel of potential jurors was enraptured. Never has a lawyer had a more attentive audience. His client was thus engaged, he said, when three island natives jumped out of the grass, beat up the poor suckee, and dragged off Deirdre X and raped her.

The criminals were not apprehended. Deirdre X's suit maintains that the Captain Kiss's Island Hotel and its conglomerate parent should have made the beach secure for the activities which led to the outrage of her person.

The Robert Redford look-alike who introduced himself as counsel for the defense also wore a brown suit with a vest: We will argue, he said, that this incident never happened, but that if it did, the Captain Kiss's Island Hotel in no way bears responsibility for the consequences of Deirdre X's life-style.

Both lawyers shamelessly argued their case to the potential jurors under the guise of providing the background we needed to determine our degree of objectivity. No judge was present, only a court officer with a little bingo drum who picked out the names of the panel members for their turn in the juror chairs. I was desperate to be called. The turnover was heavy. A single woman of the plaintiff's generation did not stand a chance of getting past the Kiss Island lawyer. None of the black men sitting could hope to pass the challenge of Dierdre X's lawyer. Nor could any women Deirdre X's mother's age. One by one, two by two, the chairs were emptied and refilled. If this case actually got into the courtroom, it would be a corker. It interested me that community standards had shifted to the degree that a woman would take the witness stand and testify to her intimate life and erotic inclinations in order to find justice. Also that a multinational conglomerate in the business of selling sex would defend itself by impugning the character of anyone who bought it. That was very interesting, I liked that a lot.

Alas, my number was not called. I took the trouble to memorize the names of the lawyers and will phone one or the other to see how things turned out. Meanwhile Deirdre X sits waiting in my mind. She is dressed in a dark business suit and a chaste white shirtwaist with a ruffled collar. Her face is scrubbed, her lips unpainted, her gaze is proud and steadfast. The sadness of her story is that she was lonely enough to be seduced by a corporation. She was debased to bare herself in the packaged sunshine of the Captain Kiss's Island Hotel. The triumph of her story is that she has found the courage to go bare-assed again, in a court of law, if that's what it takes to get justice, or at least a fair settlement, from this treacherous fantasy-husband, this advertising oversoul of a money-making machine turned rapist.

Maybe next time Deirdre will get involved with an individual, as most people do, and not expect to testify again as to her sexual nature until, having married, she sues for divorce.

A drink last night with my friend Mattingly, the rugged desert painter, who's in town for a show. It's good to be back in my own generation. He tells me he and his third wife, Mariko, are separated. Not, as I might have thought, because he has finally found the woman for his life, having searched arduously and with looming mythological stature in the gossip of artists living and dead, curators, collectors, critics, and other joyous witnesses of the prodigious; and not, as I might have suspected, because Mariko has finally given up on him, cast him out for the Faustian fornicator he has proven to be —indeed, as enamoratum of female art students across America from

Big Sur to Boston, he must have tried even her uncomplaining soul, this loyal little nisei woman with her solemn gaze and quietly elegant manner—but because she, Mariko, has undertaken an affair. She!

Mattingly is not given to wonder how uncharacteristic it may have been for his wife to do this kind of thing. He tells me it is not the affair per se that so disturbs him, but that the fellow Mariko has fallen in with is an idiot, Mattingly knows him and thinks he's an incredible fool, and that is what cannot be forgiven. So my friend has moved out of his desert home and is living in Santa Fe. In fact Mariko now wants them to get back together, but as far as he's concerned it's over. He has been irrevocably, unforgivably defamed by the poor quality of his wife's choice of lover. What does it say about one, after all, to be cuckolded by a contemptible schmuck.

Of course this is not the diction he used. Mattingly is a Western monosyllabic, which is one aspect of his great dignity. His chest is enormous from a longstanding emphysema that would by now have killed an ordinary man. The creases in his spatulate fingers are black, his nails show the dirt of the palette, and like many painters and sculptors he's essentially illiterate. You can't help but admire that. And he has done incredibly fine work, it's as if he finds the ghosts inside the people he paints, or that the rocks and mountains he likes for his subjects are broken open into some kind of elemental inner light. His paintings stand. I like and envy Mattingly, and have in the past wanted to be like him, brave in the world, daring, asking nothing of others, embracing the torments of the sojourner, living in the desert in winter, climbing the rock cliffs of one's independence. But it is ironic, he and his wife breaking up because of something *she's* done. Migod! when they lived for a spell in SoHo I remember Mariko running down the dark wooden stairs beyond the light of a loft party crying out Mattingry! Mattingry! as if seeking with her monogamous spirit to save him from the depths of his anarchies, calling out not like a jealous wife but like a guiding spirit trying to save him from his hellish plunges into self-destruction—all from her love for this man.

So we are sitting in this mock Victorian bar on Third Avenue and when he hears about my new digs he makes the same assumption everyone makes. Don't wait until you're fifty-five, he says of married men who split, do it now. I'm fifty, are there such gradations to middle age? He coughs, puts out his cigarette, and speaks in his gravelly voice of the discouragement, the despair, of being renewed through serious love, the difficulty of mounting a new life. Mariko was his third wife, and he's made children with all three, and he works like hell teaching, painting, hustling his work, just to pay his child support and his rent, he wears jeans and a frayed shirt with a string tie and a corduroy jacket and scuffed hide shoes, and he's stopped drinking, and some of that ruggedness has turned fleshy, and between the artist and simple dereliction there is a very thin line, I know that. Dereliction is the state of mind given to middle-aged men alone, not to women. Middle-aged women alone turn feisty and keep busy and become admirable characters and achieve things. They find young boyfriends. They stay clean and neat and change their hairstyle from time to time.

Would Angel ever do what Mariko did, fall in love with a man not her husband? She threatens to. Last night, my birthday, she came in with the children, and while they were out roaming the neighborhood she told me that a couple of nights before she was so desperate she actually considered going to a bar. Of course, she said after a moment, I wouldn't think of the sleazy places up where we are. It would have to be a kind of Greenwich bar, with a name like Waffle's or Titmouse's or T. S. Eliot's. While I was laughing at that, she gave me a present, a small white plastic wastebasket for my bathroom— a gift from someone who's being thrown out, is what I think she said. Oh my great troubled heart: and at night, after they had all left to go back to Connecticut, I dreamt I was in a big bedroom of many

occupied beds and on the far side of the room looking at me was
Angel. Then the image changed and another Angel, Angel S., the
publisher's wife who has been ill lately, was being affixed, nude, in
some sort of orthopedic frame, preparatory to an operation on her
heart. Her husband was the surgeon and I next saw him doing the
operation, examining with some large drill-press kind of microscope
the screwtight mechanism being implanted in her heart. And then
the image turned again and I was in the bathroom of a logging camp
with many urinals and it was crowded, and there in the open field
beyond when I tried to leave, I was menaced by psychopaths who
seemed to get in my way, threaten me, attack me. No matter which
way I turned I was in for punishment by these grotesque bullying
looming crazies whom I didn't understand and could not placate.
And then later I was seducing some young girl in my own bed, a
very erotic love scene, and there was no guilt at all.

What I did on my birthday: I cleaned this place, I'm into
housewifing, vacuuming, washing the bathroom floor. No one will
believe that I do this.

I heard from the Dark Lady with her astute timing telling me she
will leave Athens in a day or so and go on to Egypt. I am pitted
against the world.

I received a call from my mother in which she wished she was as
young as I.

I received a call from the tall Icelander who with the encourage-
ment of her covetous and luscious friend has been negotiating in
some incredible upper-class way to adore me as an Eskimo slowly,
patiently, endlessly tracks the giant white bear.

I entertained my wife and children, loving them all and taking
them for good Mexican food down the block. Nobody said, and
everybody felt, how odd this husband and father is in his own
apartment. Imagine—his having gone ahead and done this thing
without any warning or announcement. I wanted them to ask me

about it. I wanted to tell them: I am doing this to find out why I'm doing it. I wanted to assure them: after all, you kids could be visiting me in a prison, or a hospital, isn't this better, this working retreat I've made for myself in the middle of the electric city? I speak to the journey we each must make, I give you the lesson of courage in selfhood, I pray that I am in good health, I pray for us all that God grant us long life in excellent good health.

That prayer part is from something I made up one night years ago when I was unable to sleep from my good fortune. I composed this placation, this fervent invocation not to be punished for my happiness: Dear God, keep the blessings flowing, grant us all great good health and long life, with no illness, no sickness, no disease, no affliction of any kind, mental or physical. Spare us from all disasters, human or natural, and from all accidents, and spare us from violence, whether organized and official or spontaneous and haphazard. Let there be no breakdown or deterioration of any of our internal systems or organs, no loss of acuity of our senses, no diminution of our abilities and capacities. Keep our reflexes sharp. Let us live in a world of peace and social justice. Let us breathe clean air and drink pure water. Let us live in love and joy and creativity, knowing courage and finding wisdom and having a shot at enlightenment. I think that about covers everything, except extend this terrific grant to everyone I know and whoever they may have an affection for and so on, amen.

I see I left out food, you could starve to death under that grant.

I am really tired this morning. Am I on my right path or is this my ultimate act of self-hatred? When am I being true to myself and when am I only doing penance? Here's a birthday card from the MGP Capital Corporation. They shouldn't have. I see where some off-Broadway group is celebrating the Kafka centennial. Kafka would break out in a big sepulchral smile if he knew he was having a centennial. I ask the question again: Would Angel do what Mariko Mattingly did? I think yes in the event she decided or underwent the conviction that I had been unfaithful to her. Then she would be unfaithful to me. It would be an act in the interest of symmetry, like so much of what she does, a means of redressing imbalance or injustice, which is the same thing. She would do it in imitation, she would do it to be me.

Perhaps Angel's primeval urge to siamate, to speak with my voice, to think my thoughts, to use my gestures, to mingle our souls like some gloppy finger painting, is not an instinct given to all women. Catholic women? Angel is an Irish Catholic married, if tenuously, to a New York Jew. Maybe we are talking of assimilation here. Mariko, a Japanese Catholic, is married to Mattingly, a Western animist. Moira, an Irish Protestant from Chicago, is ignored by Brad, a Presbyterian columnist from Minneapolis. Jeanie, a Methodist TV producer from Asheville, wonders why she remains married to Nick, a Greek Orthodox from Philly. Rachel, a Hungarian refugee, is tormented by the red underwear of Ralph, an Ashkenazi from Brooklyn. Llewellyn, a Buddhist Welshman, is in retreat from Anne, a Quaker from Swarthmore, PA. When I walk into the Blue-bird Diner on lower Broadway the counterman gives me the gold-tooth grin. Hey, compadre, he says. He tosses me the laminated menu that you hold like choir music. The plates slap through the slot, oh chili, soup of chicken, oh pigs' feet, oh lamb stew, lasagna (homemade), fried steak and souvlaki. The food of diners is organic history, like tree rings, it is like the sea wrack of waves of migrations, the detritus of vast tidal movements of impassive populations. Shivering all night by the bronze doors of the embassy, saving their dinars, their rupees, their cruzeiros, wrapping their treasures in gray handkerchiefs, tying ropes around the brittle cane of the suitcase, jamming the buses, clambering to the rooftops of the streetcars. Infants are squeezed to death in their mothers' arms, old men give up the grasp of their bluebone hands on the gunwales and are gulped in the briny swell, young men crawl under the excoriating barbs, they ford the rivers, all of us trying to get away with the clothes on our backs, the flapping clothes on our whipped backs.

Maybe I'm right, maybe I'm wrong, maybe I'm weak, maybe I'm strong . . .

Migod, I have just found a little bump on the scrotum. No, that's not possible, I wouldn't do that to myself, would I?

It's nothing. This leathery sac, this string pouch, these lungs of sex suffering all manner of emotions, they should show some signs of wear, no? It's nothing, an arc of vein, I'll check it out from time to time. Cheggidout man, the street peddlers pointing to the gloves scarves calculators spread out on the sidewalk. Cheggidout.

So the other night we're at the Gordons', the table set for twelve, and Ginny calls us in and makes up the seating while we stand there. Why I love her: This is the crowd that buys Garland ranges for its kitchens, I mean they toss off a salmon mousse the way I heat water for coffee, well-known chefs are their weekend guests in the Hamptons. Dinner tonight is a gray water with chunks of unnameable matter floating in it. Ginny distributes it in a state of terrified hope, her beautiful eyes blinking rapidly.

Mmm, someone says, oh Ginny, someone else says, and forks are quietly laid down and the conversation becomes animated. Lloyd the cardiologist is panicked into attacking his profession: Bypass operations are epidemic, like tonsillectomies in the thirties, he says, for some reason pointing at his plate, perhaps it seems to him a tonsil lies there. Then Raoul, little Raoul, holds the table with a routine he's taking to Vegas. Raoul is beside himself trying to be brave. He goes for the wine, finds no solace: Jack Gordon, an editor for the *Times,* tonight pours a Chilean red. I look at Raoul's face and recall a dinner at his penthouse on Fifty-seventh Street, everything in shades of white, the pickled floors, the furniture. But on the walls, large color fields beautifully lit. The rooms stocked with opera stars, writers, directors, and painters of the paintings on the walls, everything and everyone a glittering marvel of Raoul's perfectionist soul, and the little host himself, running happily toward the kitchen calling Jean-Pierre! Jean-Pierre! I think we're ready now for the choucroute!

Raoul slumps back in his seat. Sitting here at Ginny's left, I kiss her cheek and sacrifice myself for the good of the community. I ask for seconds. I receive a flashing look of gratitude from Angel. I try to sop up the mess with a chunk of stale baguette. Jean-Pierre! Jean-Pierre! I think we're ready for the canned creamed corn!

At this moment, everyone assiduously not looking at his plate, a despair settles over the company. Before I know what is happening people have begun to tell stories of their muggings.

Andrea Dintenfass was hailing a taxi at the corner of Central Park West and Seventy-fourth Street in broad daylight and as the cab pulled up this tall young black man sprang to the door and held it open for her. She was somewhat startled but reasoned that he had recognized her—Andrea is a dancer with the New York City Ballet. Her husband, Moshe, is the architect. She smiled and thanked the young man; as she bent forward to enter the cab he put his hand on the middle of her back and shoved her sprawling, facedown, across the seat. He slammed the door behind her pounded the taxicab roof with the flat of his hand and shouted Move Motherfucker! And only as she struggled to a sitting position, aided by the quick acceleration of the cab, did she realize her shoulder bag was gone. He must have cut the strap, she said. It all happened so quickly, it was so brazen, done with such elegance, she said, smiling almost wistfully, not a wasted movement.

George, the wavy-haired labor lawyer, tells an ever better one: His Mercedes 300D turbo diesel is bumped from behind one Thursday night in July on the Long Island Expressway. George pulls to the side. The car behind him pulls over too, a nondescript Chevy, and several Hispanic males get out and join him in inspecting the damage. George and the Hispanics are all hunkering down between the two cars, the heavy traffic is going by, a tunnel of flared light and blue exhaust, and only his car is damaged, a dent, a broken light, and he is expressing his irritation and they are nodding sympathetically, and then he notices one of them holding a small snub-nosed pistol in the palm of his hand. George finishes what he has to say. He is politely relieved of his wallet, his watch, his tie clip, and while he hunkers there as he's been instructed, one of the men has gotten in behind the wheel of his Mercedes and another has walked up to the window where George's wife, Judy, is sitting, and together they persuade her to turn over her jewelry her purse her cosmetic case. They grab the stereo tapes, they take the luggage from the trunk of the car, pocket the turbo diesel's keys, get back into their Chevrolet, whose license plate is caked with mud, and, with one of them standing in the slow lane to hold up traffic, they indolently pull back on the road and moments later they're nothing but a pair of red lights in the great expressway light show.

Today on the subway: *Efecto seguro! No más suciedad; no más fastidio; no más cucarachas! Johnson's No Roach—efecto rápido, un tratamiento dura varios meses.* The good Don tipping his lance in Johnson's No Roach, mounting his knacker and setting off to the fray. The impassive heads sitting in line shaking in unison as the express rocks through the tunnel. The impassive inundation at Fourteenth Street. We are each aloof in our private beings, our cilia wigglingly alert to those closest to us because they may without warning do us harm. My skin is my border. I may read a newspaper, but I can't think, I'm conscious of them, they flow through me, the presence of impassive strangers flows through me and shoulder to shoulder, bottom halves carefully untouching, we form in the thirty seconds between stations momentary grudging community, all dissolved and reformed as the doors open, some of us jam out and new impassivities jam in.

I grew up underground, why do I feel out of place? Cheggidout man, white dude, glasses, face too soft, in these years under your stationary flight path great migrations breasted the sea, dug through the mountains, rode the tectonic plates. You thought refugees meant Jews but it never stopped, the doors fly open, new generations of impassivities tumble in, and I am as strangled in history as this little old lady in her fur hat and blond wig and delicate white skin, this Jewish grandma with prim distaste stomping the people in front of her to get to the door.

The car empties. Now we are idlers in a café on a slow evening, I find a seat a moment later, a young black man, I look up from my reading, he holds the strap with one hand with the other holds under my face a fedora filled with coins and bills. What is he saying? His right pants leg is rolled above the knee, the leg is prosthetic, he displays for my pleasure his manikin leg, give him money quick, a medal pinned to the hat brim, I'll pay I'll pay, he twists on the strap, topples to the other side of the car, grabs the strap there, an aerialist, not a coin has spilled, the back of his knee is open I see the steel shaft and socket, this is no scam, this is a legitimate hustle. He works the car one stop, two, it crowds up again and he gets off.

And what is this: poised at the open door to the platform unable to make up his mind for the express, a gringo in a black car coat, prison-gray trousers, space shoes. What the hell, he says, they's too many, I'll never make it, I'll fall on the tracks, you think they care, you think they give a good goddamn? No one in this world gives a doodlyfuck, am I right? He asks this of no one, he needs no one, migod, *now* I feel at home on the subway, an audible brain, a mind wired for broadcast, I move up behind him, his scrawny neck is pitted with black shot, tufts of black hair sprout from his ears. The express roars in, the impassive crowd bunches on the platform ready to spring. He says in the door of the local, You gotta be fucking crazy

to fight that mob! But, why not, what the hell, I'm as good as them
. . . He saunters out. Follow that man! You know how valuable he
is? He's as old as the dragonfly, he was here before the caves of
Lascaux. This antediluvian artist is my ancestor, he invented me.

A hurled rain, coming in gusts at a slant, like flung seed. Shows
you what the wind looks like. Hits the adjoining high-rise and
plunges like a cataract. The swings flinging about in the playground.
The sky over Houston is white-gray, and something's missing, the
World Trade Center, it's gone, erased. The skyline now is no higher
than the 1930's, the era of my birth, this gets any heavier we'll be back
in the last century with Melville's ironfronts. Cobblestones. Mayan
reservoirs. I've opened the sliding window a crack to give it a voice.
I can barely hear the churchbell in this roar. But wait, splashing
across the street, bowed but, just as it says over the portals of the main
post office on Eighth Avenue, undeterred by rain, sleet or any other
shit, here he comes, the big shoulder bag looking like a humpback
under his poncho.

Well let's see what I have for his labor: Would I sign a letter
protesting the coming Polish show trials against Solidarity activists?
I would. Would I put my name down as a sponsor for the upcoming
nuclear freeze poetry reading? Sure. And Christ, look at this, Hubbard's Cave in Warren County Tennessee the most important bat
cave in North America according to Dr. Merlin Tuttle, international
authority on these flying mammals: Unless the Conservancy finds
twenty thousand bucks to ensure the protection of the cave, a hiber-
nating colony of one hundred and fifty thousand rare gray bats could
be wiped out.

Shrieky little things. Teeth like glazier points. Gummy eyes.
White bellies. Wing skin. Shit a lot. Doc, let me think about it, O.K.?

And here, one drop of the rainstorm like a splashed tear running
the lavender ink, a picture card from Egypt. A huge stepped temple

on the Nile. *This is the size of the feeling*, it says in her hand, and *this is the specific location of the heart.*

Gulp.

We communicate intimately over great distances. We warrant ourselves. I feel a calm resolution of being, I feel as if I'm holding her in my arms.

But of course happiness is intolerable for more than two seconds. What if I'm too old for her? We'll no sooner move in together than I'll come down with Alzheimer's disease. You think that's funny? The other day those Willie and Joe strips of World War II came to my mind, those beautifully drawn panels of GI life. I couldn't remember the name of the artist. I even knew that after the war he drew political cartoons for the St. Louis *Post-Dispatch*. Bill something. Then it came to me as slow as a pinball bumping its way down to the slot, or like an ancient computer byte blinking through a thousand weak glimmering tubes. Mauldin. That's not funny at all. The other day I poured a drink, put the glass on the bar, and sat down on the sofa with the bottle. The shower head fools me every time—I no sooner step under it than I hear the phone ringing. I see the moon through the trees and it turns out to be a street lamp. I'm flaking away. Christ. If you can't name, you're not human. The simplest thing, which corner to turn two blocks from home, can leave you as eerily as a hundred fifty thousand gray bats flooping out of Hubbard's Cave.

I've got to do some heavy working out, I've got to get in shape, plan a regimen for myself, heavy cardiovascular stuff. You keep the arteries supple, and everything else takes care of itself, am I right? I'll slow my growing old until she catches up to me, until we're running right along together. I'll be her age for her, that's what my love can do. Starting tomorrow.

And now I have to think of what happened to Riordan when *he* fell in love. I did a reading at his campus and stayed at his home. In the early hours of the morning, after the party, we had one last drink and he told me. Riordan has published a half-dozen novels. None of them have made money but he's doing all right, he's gotten his grants and manages to keep going. A few years ago he was on track for tenure at a good little school down south. He was married, happily, if calmly, and didn't expect it or look for it, but all at once he was in love with a woman he had met a few times at parties, the wife of a dean or director of admissions. And she fell in love with him. So there they were, a total of five young kids between them, his three, her two, and they couldn't get enough of each other. He portrayed her as a tremblingly sensual woman, a kind of head-tossing being not born for the conventions of middle class. She was a sculptor given to pieces showing the heads of birds on human bodies. Or vice versa. He never described her but I imagined her as somewhat full-hipped, with big boobs, real shifters. He met her in the afternoons, and it didn't go away, the more they saw of each other the more intense it became. He rented a small room miles from the campus and he would read to her in bed the work she had inspired—the best he'd ever done before or since, he insisted, a rhythmic, energetic prose, the voice of his courage, is the way he put it. She in her turn realized in her love for him that she had been asleep most of her life. She was fervent in her feeling. She called his love her redemption.

Finally it became apparent to them that there was nothing else to do but for each of them honorably to announce their relationship, make full confession to their spouses, give up custody of their children and leave town. He would resign his job and they would make a new life together in some other part of the country. If he could swing an advance from his publisher they might even live abroad. There was nothing they could not do.

And so at the end of the semester the day came. He posted his letter of resignation and sat his poor wife down in the living room of their home. He told her everything except his lover's name. She was shocked, stunned, devastated—she had had no idea. She was a good simple girl, he said, quite pretty in her own frail way, a loyal loving wife, actually, he said, except that before he could get out of the house she had turned insane and, as he ran, clipped him on the back of the head with a heavy pot of pompons he didn't know she had the strength to lift, let alone heave.

Somewhat woozy, probably suffering a mild concussion, Riordan drove off to his rendezvous. The lovers had surreptitiously packed bags for themselves days before, and all the belongings they wanted were already in the trunk of the car—even some of his books, even a couple of her smaller pieces. He waited for her in the appointed place, the parking lot behind a supermarket.

He waited and waited. She was late but this was characteristic of her and he didn't worry although his head was aching. A pickup truck drove into the lot and pulled up alongside him. A student got out and asked him if he was Professor Riordan, and when he nodded the student handed him a letter, said, Have a nice day, Professor, and drove off. He opened the letter. He had immediately recognized her hand, her large romantic scrawl, in the same green ink and on the same gray vellum that had given him revelation of life's wild fulfillments: I cannot tell my husband, the letter said. I can't bear to leave my children. I will love you always. I hope someday you will forgive me.

Riordan told this story quietly. He smoked cigarettes and mashed them out in the ashtray. He was married again—to neither of the women in the story, but a pleasant-enough person, I thought, who said when we were introduced how much she liked my work. She looks a lot like Riordan—slender, fair, light-haired, with pink-rimmed eyes. Freckles. No children.

On the other hand, what could be more dangerous than twenty years of marriage, where she has the same thought a few seconds after you have it, or before; or that you tell her one day how fragile your ego is, how you keep drifting in and out of yourself and don't remember who you are supposed to be, and she tells you she has the same experience, disappearing into herself, and so the two of you have been living together all these years not sure of who you are or what you're supposed to feel, but known to one and all as the same clear couple they've always known and recognized, a flowerpot on the back of the skull may be preferable.

Fifties update!

Ralph of the red underwear is still not sleeping with his wife, Rachel, although his affair is over. He knows from his analysis, to which he has submitted himself five days a week, that Rachel strongly resembles his dead mother. We walk the streets as he tells me this, he stares at the ground, he holds his hands behind his back as he walks, we are two good and gentle burghers on our *Spaziergang* while youths amble by with their ghetto blasters and women blowing bubble gum sway past us on white roller skates. It's not Rachel's fault, Ralph says. How can I tell her, my wife, a survivor of the Holocaust, that she symbolizes death?

And stern Sascha, who told me to get in or get out, has left his wife, Mary. It comes as no surprise. Last winter Angel and I went with them to Barbados. I'm not crazy about the Caribbean but the two women had conspired—Mary wanted to be alone with Sascha for a few days but she had no hope of getting him down there on her own. We settled into a pleasant routine, reading on the beach, bathing, tennis in the late afternoon, a good dinner at night. But a few days into it Mary began to come unstrung. If my husband doesn't make love to me soon I'm going to walk into the ocean, she told Angel. So one night after the ladies had retired I had a brandy with Sascha at the hotel bar. We had started on rum at about five and had polished off a couple of bottles of good wine at dinner, and we were both fairly well along. Sosh, I said, there's an implicit agreement in a Caribbean holiday, you can't bring a woman to a place like this and not fuck her. Even your wife. He rose to his feet with such drunken resolution that the chair he'd been sitting in fell over backward. Of course you're right, Jonathan, he said, and hitching up his trousers, he staggered off.

But the scandalous news is Brad: First night back in town after his trip to the Middle East, Brad was seen at Elio's with his wife, Moira. I feel the ground sliding from under me.

Angel's incessant theme, that I never relax, relent, go with something, that it's always a matter of principle, it's always a big urgent issue, nothing is forgiven, forgotten, nothing is small or unimportant. That is correct. She on the other hand has no pride and would not think of turning down an invitation no matter how surely loathsome the company. She has been doing this to me for years. I simply won't go. She is intimidated by the most casual social demands, God will strike her dead if she says no. If she feels she is accepted, she will crawl on the rocks in the sun in the dust of the desiccated shit of armadillos.

My father rode the subway. I remember once walking him to the subway station, he went to work ten, eleven in the morning, catching the D train to get downtown to his accounts: Be nice to your mother, try to cooperate, don't do anything to upset her. How I loved him. The man who disappointed millions. Make promises, fail to keep them. Give your assurances, forget them. Give you his raging wife. I am maybe thirteen. They have had a battle and he's leaving me behind to cool her out. All day I will dread the night. She will make dinner in silence, serve three plates, and she and I will dine. My father's dinner will sit there. She will not touch it. I do my homework, go to sleep. In the early morning I awaken to another engagement: Where has he been, what has he done? The curses, the accusations, the physical attack. He will defend himself and hurt her and she will cry and I will be there in my pajamas trying to make the peace between them, screaming at them both at three A.M.

I would wake up to these terrible sounds of struggle, blows, cries, I didn't know whom to believe, whom to love, whom to defend, whom to attack, I felt this sick pleasure not knowing what I felt, hearing these sounds.

Today my mother is eighty-six, bent, arthritic, with evidence in scars of three or four heart attacks which she was too strong to feel when she had them. She has had an operation for cancer. She has mottled old woman's skin, she has trouble walking, she has arteriosclerosis, a herniated esophagus, and glaucoma. And all her marbles. I didn't understand your father, she says now. He was a wonderful man, he had a fine mind. He did not think like anyone else. I didn't understand that, I tried to make him like everyone else.

My father's been dead thirty years. Had he lived longer, he might have seen the dawn of that beneficent judgment.

I met him when I was sixteen, my mother will tell me. We went ice skating at Crotona Park. He was so dashing, so handsome. He wouldn't let me go out with another boy. In the spring he brought me flowers. We played tennis. He was a wonderful tennis player. Mama didn't want me to marry him.

That's the fellow. Made things happen, my pop. He could get through police lines, talk his way past any stage doorman on Broadway. Come up with tickets to the sold-out concert at Carnegie Hall. Get us into the game. He made occasions of the simplest things—a walk in the park, a picnic outing. He had ideas, he gave us books to read, brought home movie cameras, electric trains, pulled things out of his hat. He got us through the Depression! Yet his life is said to have been a failure. There is a mythology of his failure. His wrong business decisions, and errors of judgment continue to obsess us more than twenty-five years after his death. That's why my brother finds it so hard to part with money, why my mother has no one to her house, why I always rush to pay the bills, my share, more than my share, a penance for my success, the impertinence of it.

As a young bank teller, it is said, he was extremely handsome, and so caught the eye one day of a man who arrived at the polished marble counter wearing a beret, and a pince-nez. This was a film director, it is said, a European then putting together a series of motion pictures about a daring female beauty who each week at the nickelodeon would be left in some terrible precarious position from which only next week's installment would rescue her. Her name was Pearl White and an appropriately heroic good-looking young man was needed to play her rescuer and chaste companion. My father thought it over and said no. He thought he had a good career ahead of him in banking. My Jewish father. As an aspiring ensign he trained for his commission at the Webb Naval Academy on the Harlem River, but the Great War ended before his training did. I have on my wall his browned photograph, he leans on a mop handle, one of a line of swabbies with mops and pails. Gradually he accumulated wrong decisions, frustrated intentions. He went into the record business in the early thirties, the days of 78rpm shellac records, and he really knew music and his stock reflected this, and many of the reigning artists of the day ordered their records from him; but his partner pulled a fast one or two, and the business went down and my father lost his store. It was in the old Hippodrome Building on Sixth Avenue between Forty-third and Forty-fourth streets. He made a few dollars during the war, importing this and that, little business schemes, inventions by crazy Swiss tinkerers, a new kind of soap dish to keep the soap from turning gloppy, to extend its life. Soap was hard to come by in World War II, but by the time my father marketed these little devices the war was over, soap and everything else was plentiful, people wanted to waste it, the idea was to make up for the years of austerity and go through everything as fast as you could. A man wanted my father to be partners in a new venture in the record business in anticipation of the long-playing record. This time my father saw the possibilities, made the right decision, but couldn't raise the ten thousand or so he needed to buy in. You get the picture? He lost money at cards because he thought he was a good card player and he wasn't. He was always late, late going to work as a salesman for an appliance jobber, late coming home. He was a philanderer, my brother said to me one day. He had a girlfriend. Only one? The one my brother thinks of was a singer, some light soprano who had an album and wrote on the cover: To Jack, Always. But why would he bring it home if Always meant anytime? Perhaps he had no other place to bring it. He had nothing. Toward the end of his life he took to washing the dishes, cleaning the kitchen, shopping for the week's groceries. He didn't want to work anymore. When he died he was king of a three-room apartment in the Bronx where he had sat in the bathroom and read the newspapers to escape life's incremental judgments. He owned a few suits, a watch or two that didn't work, a garnet ring, an insurance policy the entire value of which he'd borrowed on. He left some white-on-white shirts, a few Sulka ties of which he was proud, an old wood tennis racket.

I turn away to the window. Downstairs, on the roof of the university sports center, the joggers in their shorts over sweatpants in their separate rhythms around the track. All over the city they run, little headphones on their ears. Once I thought they were in training for the time when there would be nothing left but to run, but that is too logical an idea. They not only run but stop in the park, lay down their briefcases, and wave their arms and kick their feet in the air. They ride unicycles with their earphones on their heads, they dance on roller skates on the abandoned highway, and in studios all over the city they attach themselves at great expense to machines that move their limbs for them. We could be picking tubers from the fields, stomping grapes, we could be running rickshas, carrying loads of faggots gathered from the forest floor.

A call from my mother: *What's the matter, did you forget I exist?*

That's the lady. Mystical, isn't it? I was just thinking of you, I say. She tells me the story of her latest triumph at the senior citizens' center. How she put some woman *in her place*. She is a good story-teller. She thinks narratively and comes to judgment through stories. When she talks about Angel, whom she likes and admires, I see Angel more appreciatively. My mother is connoisseur of the characters of women. The universe in her mind is women. These days her most intense relationship is with the young woman we hired to come in and take care of her six days a week. Periodically, she asks me to fire this woman, Toinette is her name, a Brazilian in her twenties, but when I say O.K. she tells me not to. What difference does it make, they're all alike, she explains. She has gotten Toinette to keep the house, cook things the way she likes them, wash her clothes, her hair. Every day if the weather is right they go to lunch together at some sandwich place in the neighborhood. Upper West Side. She is very regal-looking, my mother, with white hair, blue half-blind eyes, and she plays verbal games with the counterman, who asks her for dates, that sort of thing. Toinette endures this stony-faced, she endures it all, but sometimes gives expression to the feeling that comes of being in my mother's presence thirty-five hours a week. Do you know what Toinette did the other day? my mother asks me, laughing happily: She started to dance around me and make obscene gestures. I said that's really good, Toinette, you could go to Las Vegas with an act like that. Once, apparently, Toinette withdrew an ice pick from her bag, removed the wood sheath and showed it to her. She carries it in case she's attacked, at least that's what she said —I didn't let on how frightened I was, I said to her: Toinette, that's a lethal weapon, if the police find that in your possession you'll be arrested. Toinette tells my mother stories of friends of hers in the custodial health business who get so mad at the inmates in their care in the old people's homes that they step on their toes and break them.

But she won't tell me the names of the homes, my mother says. I'm wise to you, she says, you'll call up and get them fired.

All this has made my mother healthier and happier than she's been in years. Ever since this woman came to work for her, she's stopped going to the doctor.

It's her mother who had spells, we never had another name for it, my grandma with her spells, a frail little woman too, not a sturdy sort like my mother, she'd hug the good little boy one day, give him a penny and bless his head and kiss him, and curse him out the next, hose him down with a stream of vile curses in Yiddish. My grandma would come down the front steps in her black lace-up shoes and I'd be playing with my friends in front of my house and she'd shake her fist at me. Walk down the block and come back to shake it some more. Finally she'd disappear around the corner, still ranting. She ran away all the time, the cops would have to find her and bring her back.

And look at this coming down Eighth Street: his black garrison cap blocked like the old SS, his black leather jacket with raised chrome studs, his black jeans and boots. Hopping to keep up with him is a skinny androgyne, with a gold ring in his ear and a lime-green jumpsuit. Stroll theater, people cruise for the impact of themselves, it's their art form. Raster blasting, mincing, prancing, slinking the display of themselves. I go to a Mexican restaurant the other night, no one there is over twenty-five, at one table a boy and girl have identical skeezix haircuts, they sit with their arms on the table and point their hair at each other. It may be passing me by, it may all be passing me by. On the BMT the other day a young Korean comes into the car and he's carrying a chair, some sort of upholstered dining-room chair, and it's covered in polyurethane wrap, he's using the subway for haulage, a very Oriental solution somehow redolent of baskets balanced on poles over the shoulders, of ten thousand people with shovels, of the hand-digging of bomb shelters—but the kicker is the car being full, the Korean looks around, plants his chair in the middle of the floor and sits down on it. That making do, that inevitable logic of life's teeming struggle, of simple squatting accommodation.

And Hispanic young girls wheeling their babies in strollers into the subway cars, whole families piling in bag and baggage everything they own in the world, the doors can't close, this car is so packed with *compañeros*.

Down Broadway at night the feeling quite different, gangs of prepubescents holding their combs as crucifixes, or lighting each other's cigarettes importantly as they wait under the marquees for the opening of the new dismemberment movie. Knots of Nordic tourists, big doughy families, moving along too stunned to talk. Glossy girlies from the 1930's still willing to dance one flight up, the hot winds of the pizza oven gust up the trash on the sidewalks, a cop in his powder-blue plastic helmet posting as his horse trots in that sidelong way of police horses, this is the historic city of yellow cabfleets, my father knew these precincts, their flashing windows of porno, the corner hot-dog stands where whores and hustlers have their coffee break, the triple-X movie stills with the nipples and cunts blacked out, camera shops, shoe stores, the little paper umbrellas and lead Statues of Liberty, the arcades now wired for videoblast sound effects, it's war in there, but you can still buy a front page with your name in the headline. Broadway has always been a sump, nothing new here, the boopedoop sirens, the fast frisk against the wall, the cop dressed worse than the guy whose arm he has twisted up behind him as far as it'll go. The moving computer-graphic signs, the giant pantyhosed girl in the sky, the young god in briefs, the archetypes of the Great White Way. That's not what I mean.

Going to Connecticut there's, invariably, a reentry problem. I return with amnesia and a hopeful resolve, I smell the wet leaves, I see the stand of white birch in the woods behind the house, I take a deep breath of self-purification, and I get waylaid. Angel can practice civility with the deadliness of an Englishman. But that's just one of the ways. I cannot bring anything, flowers, bread from a real New York bakery, because it symbolizes the situation as she sees it. This last time she told me after the children went upstairs and we were drinking our Swiss-water-process decaffeinated coffee, how the night before she'd been to dinner down the road at the Millays': All the husbands were there except mine. I felt like a charity case. Everyone in these woods is a writer, but you're the only one who can't work here. That's right, I said. How can any of these guys get any thinking done? What do they do when they want to go for a walk? She looked at me. I've got nobody to talk to. I'm lonely. Even when you're here I'm lonely, even when you're here. You live inside your neurosis. I'm tired of not being precious to anybody. Nobody ever wonders what's doing with *me*!

And then the beautiful eyes brimmed over and she was gone from the room.

I think of cities on the water, mossy Venice with its canals of cold murk, the first Disneyland. I think of London, the wide river, the flat anarchic landscape, looming industrial white sky; or Hamburg with its estuary coming right up to the flag-decked square with the clean park, the tourist launches, my fine hotel with its bowed windows, Germans in crowds as usual; or I think of Stockholm, every foot of the archipelago channeled in stone, the palace hedged in scaffolds, construction cranes swinging about like royal attendants; or filthy overdone Paris, the water in the Seine overfished, over-pissed, now something else besides water, the air too, overbreathed, something else now not air, this ultimate metro transmuted in its own density to something else, something stopped and monumental.

I will tell Angel simply that it may not be in my nature to be married and she'll look at me, my wife of two decades, the father of her children, and I'll say there is an evolved being and eventually it declares itself. And not just to me but to you too, I am saying we must make the whole journey, it is the only justification for any of us, after the imperatives have been met—to let go, take the risk, it is the only honor and the only redemption of the last free years. And true, I have a particular hope in mind but I know what a wild hope it is, I cannot compete for her forever. And I know that. I see the stunned Mattingly wandering around trying to find a woman he can talk to, I see my friend Leonard, whose wife of fifteen years left him for a woman—he has his colleagues in for drinks in his dark new little apartment—and I see the small spaces men end up with for their lives, and there is terror, and the disgusted reproach of children, and the lapse into dereliction of men who have taken down their establishments, and I know I risk all that. I risk the drab common fate. But look, I'll tell her, if we do this right we can save of ourselves and our relationship what is good about it, we can be colleagues, we are still partners in parenthood, we can help each other, relate as real human beings, share our thoughts, maintain our regard for each other, maybe we can even go to bed from time to time.

A call from a new El Salvadoran benefit group: Would I come to hear an American doctor who works with the rebels? That interests me—the doctor flew bombing missions in Vietnam.

Hi, says my neighbor just now, meeting me at the incinerator. I heard your typewriter going this morning, you were on a real roll, weren't you?

When dusk comes this time of year the lights are already on in all of the apartments and I see several floors of action simultaneously. He is playing the piano while one floor below in the identical spot she waters a potted plant. People when talking on the phone gesticulate as if the person at the other end were right there, perhaps the body movement is necessary for the inflection. One young girl has just lifted her skirt and looked into her underpants. Children, I notice, have rooms filled with primary colors, they are said to need cheerful enameled toys, little kid there stands on the windowsill, his body pressed up against the window, arms over his head, he's looking for his dad to come home. Get down, kid. And all over the complex the TV sets shine their colors synchronously, this is a popular program, the light shifts, colors flick everywhere on every floor, a news program, look how the scenes change, the light shading, brightening, darkening, some war in green hills, people running, colors shifting.

Today was one of those unaccountably warm winter days, a teasing of spring, and everyone was out, the streets were filled, people carrying their coats, everyone popping up in the street like crocuses. A whole Dixieland band on Sixth Avenue, a black ventriloquist with a black dummy holding down a good crowd at Columbus Circle, peddlers of pistachio nuts and dried fruit everywhere, side by side with the carts of chestnuts on pans of coal. Brisk business at the boards of chess hustlers and three-card montetistas. On University Place I see a crowd, I come up to the edge, straining my neck, and it's some guy sawing a board of number-one pine, he's concentrating on his job, sawing a piece of wood for a job he's doing on a storefront, and oh my great and wonderful city a crowd has gathered to watch this man saw this board.

In the mail a letter from Seattle—my friend, the poet Rosen. Would I write some recommendations for his son who's applying to college? Incidentally, he says, whatever happened to *Lives of the Poets*? I've been promising it for a long time. Rosen hasn't published anything new lately, he feels neglected, he feels someone should be doing something to celebrate him. Oh what a stolidly irrefutable sense of himself has the good Roze, he even breathes like a king, each breath a prolonged sigh of tragic resignation, a long sorrowful expiration of hope, if breathing were poetry he would be preeminent, the Shakespeare of our age. He's short, powerfully built, very aggressive

in games, proud of his tennis and his chess. And it's true his problems
are monumental: For years he suffered a neck-to-toes case of psoriasis
that forced him to live, Marat-like, in the bathtub. He could not
endure consciousness without bathing in a potion several hours a
day. Red and crusty, splitting open like baked rock, he looked like
the planet Mars. Among poets he was as famous for his skin as for
his work. Then he learned that at the University Medical Center, a
very avant-garde research hospital, they had conceived of a new
cure. So he offered himself as a pilot study. They had him swallow
some sort of chemical and put him under ultraviolet light and they
cleared him up. He began to have hope for his life. He went to
another department where they were working on how to put together broken eardrums—he had been deaf in one ear ever since the
sixties, when he'd lost the eardrum in a riot. He'd been a passionate
contentious activist poet, always getting in trouble with the authori-
ties, getting busted for actions, clubbed on the street. Those were the
days he dressed in dashikis and peace medals and wore his black
bushy hair in an Isro. The doctors injected some sort of foam into
the inner ear which linked the broken pieces of eardrum and hardened into a whole. By this means Rosen's hearing was restored. Little
by little he was putting himself back together.

Rosen was married to Remini, an herbalist and a mystic, which
was all right in the sixties but around the time he was regaining his
health she became a disciple of a man who was the Earth Delegate
to the Council of the Cosmos, an organization of intergalactic deities
intent on teaching mankind the error of its ways. Rosen was not
sympathetic to deities. By the time his epidermis and eardrum were
back in one piece his marriage was flying apart in all directions, like
the cosmos. I liked Remini. She was an extremely tall woman with
straight blond hair, pale blue eyes, the haunches of a starving mon-
grel dog, and the sweetest smile in the world. She moved into a
downstairs room in their house and slept on a mattress on the floor.

She had a Japanese lantern in there and wall hangings from Nepal and incense candles. There was also living in the house a parolee from the local state prison. Rosen had been teaching a poetry-writing course on the inside, and recognizing this convict's literary gifts, he'd worked an early release for him and enrolled him in college. While Rosen was off teaching, Remini and this fellow lit incense together and meditated in her room. I met him once, a sly-looking fellow, body lean and sinewy, like hers, and a clear pride in him for having worked the little ten-cent device, metaphor, that had sprung him from the slammer.

Today Rosen's hair is nearly gone and what is left he cuts close. He wears blue blazers and ties. He shares his life with a lovely lady his own height. Their children get along. He coaches the Little League team his younger son plays on, he wants to win, he wants to do things right and win, but though he's done some translating, he hasn't written anything of his own that satisfies him in many years now, his skin is clear, his tennis is good, he beats his computer at chess but he hasn't written much to speak of.

And what have we here, an urgent communication from my phone company: *Estimado Cliente, si no paga la cantidad completa, y nos es necesario interrumpir su servicio, no tendremos otra alternativa que cancelar su cuenta.* You stupid spick computer, I paid my bill!

What I want for my life now is for it to be simple, without secrets, I want to be who I really am with everyone, all the time. I want the person I love to be the person I make love to. I experience love, or love of her, as a state of clarity, of coming into being. There is a coincidence of who I am and who I ought to be. And I told her this once, I told her I thought of her as my natural wife because I had never felt this with anyone, this sense of having arrived finally in my life. And of course you find silly romantic signs, but it is true that I draw a good deal, have always drawn—faces usually, animals, cars, planes, sometimes my own hand, but over the years one face, in profile, since I was a boy I've drawn that face and it turned out to be' hers. I proved this to her one day by drawing it without looking at her and it was she, the same forehead, nose, the same serene brow, raised exquisite lips, strong chin, large clear eye. And surely I didn't do this to her, that you can read my phone number on the license plate of her car. I didn't invent that. But the willingness to find these things is love.

I have the courage to give up everything for her. I'm not making it a condition of our relationship that you leave your wife, she said once in a panic. She may lack daring. She may not love danger. *Yet why not say what happened?* Lowell's line. All right, I know I'm in trouble, I've had to force this affair, she does not naturally take to it. Once she said by way of justifying her doubts: For the longest time I didn't feel I was specific enough to you. I protested. No, she said, I think you wanted to be in love.

She is not jealous or possessive yet I read in this remark a reference to the unfortunate beginning of our relationship. I was instantly, enormously overwhelmed by her, dazzled beyond belief, yet I went off with her friend—an impulsive jock move of the moment, I later said by way of explanation when months afterward I finally called her. I had met them together one summer weekend. I wanted you, I said, and thought you couldn't possibly be free. I sent my arrow as close as I could get it.

And the intensity of feeling misdirects us, I know this to be so, Rilke fell in love with two women who were friends. He married one and continued to love the other. It is said of our own Moira, passionately sufferingly married to Brad, that just before she eloped with him she told her old boyfriend that she would marry him if he still wanted her. There is such radiance in us when we love—our gyro careens, wobbles, threatens to dump us right out of the universe. It seems to me not unusual that, in the wild blare of absolute ecstatic conviction of love for a woman, in your jumped vivacity, you could just as easily reach for the woman standing next to her.

Yet here she is roaming the world, taking the time to think about us and think about what she wants to do. Greece, Egypt, India . . . Christ, how much time does she need, I haven't got all day. She's already told me she loves me and is terrified. They fear being claimed, this generation. How ridiculous. She's got her own career, she's got her Dickens, her Hardy, her James, she teaches dead writers, such an appalling profession that I would despair of doing anything about it. What terrifies me is that she will want us to be friends. This has always been her instinct. And it's easy and blessed enough, I know, I understand Ruskin, I understand all the chaste nineteenth-century passions of the drawing room, those triumphs of unceasing love of spinsters for curates, of scholars for their cousins, and it's true, it can be sustained without sticking a stumpy polyp of yourself into the gap of someone else. The love conducted by platonists is safer and less troubled, it never stands corrected, you are fixed in the firmament and nothing can shake you, you exist in the shining orb of each other's moral regard and whatever each of you does with your body, and with whom, is of no consequence. And it may be in her nature to love only that way, she never married, she's what, thirty, thirty-one, she's had the men she's wanted one way or another since she was fifteen, one of the last of the flower children, she rode on their motorcycles, she did mescaline on the beach with them, she lived once with a dealer, once even with another writer, and it has always broken up in a matter of months—six months, I think she said, was the longest she was ever with anyone.

Eighteen years is the longest I've ever been with anyone.

And I admit I'm not possessive in my feelings, I am persuaded to sophistication by her independent life. I like to make you come, I said to her one night. But that's my responsibility, she said. She is remarkably lovely. She has the body I've given to heroines in my work: small-breasted, narrow-waisted, a big behind. She is not a woman who cries easily. She is calm, her voice is beautiful, without complaint in it, without a self-demeaning note. I give to her a serenity, a poise in the world which she insists she doesn't have. But what does she know? She has been matter-of-factly promiscuous all her life yet thinks of herself as a lonely spinsterish drab who works all day lecturing and marking papers and sits down alone with a ritual martini in the evening to watch a movie on television.

What's going on on Houston Street? It's raining, and lit by the amber street lamp in front of the Mobil gas station are four eight twelve parked taxicabs, one half of them on the sidewalk. Their lights are off but the drivers sit inside, every once in a while a match flares. More yellow cabs pull up behind, alongside, and now the headlights of two suddenly go on and the motors start and they drive away, tires squealing and the cabs behind them move up and wait, in their turn, to take off. I get my binoculars. The amber raindrops falling past my eyes. The cab doors are all the same escutcheon, one company. Cabs parked in the rain with their lights out on a big-money night? It's cops. Three of them pull out now and race east down Houston. I know they use these dummy cabs to bust car rings. Car thieves are organized, they can get an automobile into the shop and take it apart in five minutes, or down to the docks and in the ship's hold and it's halfway across the ocean the next morning. The cops can't get near them in patrol cars, even unmarked cars, they use cabs to get the jump. So that's what I'm seeing. But this operation in the rain looks more like heavy surveillance, something big, a big-money crop in SoHo. They hang a right at Broadway.

I don't know. Duplicity in individuals is, of course, the basis of civilization, but the double life of state agencies, cops as cabdrivers, cops as bag ladies, cops as tourists—that is schizy, it's tribal theater, it taps into existential energies, it releases hot mysterious powers. I like my cops in uniforms with badge numbers I can read, I like police departments with budgets argued at public hearings. Officers, detectives, should be neatly dressed and easily identified. I don't want them in fantasy drag, with their cover stories and secret files. Who knows what they believe as they mole among us?

Sidney, the agent, who is a black belt and said to have run arms for the Irgun many years ago, once said to me: It's Jews like me who watch over Jews like you.

But I claim you have the means here of cross-wiring reality—a sputter, a high-voltage sponk, and the neurons blow. My friend Gary, age fifty, runs his own public-relations firm and prominently contributes to Democratic Party campaigns. When I was close to him he was married to Abigail, it was a second marriage for both. This is pertinent. They each had a child from the previous marriage and had together produced three. After the third, Abigail requested of Gary that he submit himself to a vasectomy. He was reluctant to do this, being testosterone-proud like all of us, but in the interest of their relationship he put himself in the hospital and had it done. That relaxed the tension between them and everything was fine except that some months afterward he found in Abigail's purse a plastic case molded like a sea shell and you know what comes in those things. But this would be of no more consequence than any other sad song of love except for Gary's view of the matter, which he confided in a lowered voice at the bar of Wally's a few months after his divorce: It was when I saw her diaphragm, he said, that I knew Abigail was CIA.

I thought he was insane. I remember treating him somewhat rudely. Come on, Gary, I said, what makes you think the CIA would want *you* for a husband? But now I think his remark among the most prophetic it has ever been my privilege to hear uttered. To discover your wife fucking someone else is one thing, but to be betrayed by the United States government is quite another. Think of it as a metaphor and it will begin to work for you as it has worked for me. Think of Gary as a poet. In one brief moment of tortured inspiration he pulled in the *Zeitgeist* as a sail fills with the wind. I know guys writing all their lives who will never come close to it.

At Josie's dinner last night: She tells us her younger child came home with a mimeographed letter from the headmaster, a sort of psychological alert, advising the parents of Mulberry School that on the sidewalk in front of the main entrance, that morning, some of their children may have had the experience of seeing a dead man who happened to be lying there. We all laugh merrily. Paul, who was a city reporter in his younger days, explains you see stiffs now on the street because the cops won't investigate if they find them there. Which is not the case if they find a body inside a building. They become detectives then. So the joker OD's, his friends and relatives take his wallet, cut the labels off his rags, and carry him out at night and lay him down with the ash cans. No problem.

Before realizing it we are going around the table with dead-man stories and that would be all right except one of the guests, Marvin, the wealthy publishing heir and bachelor, is terminal, he's got maybe six months. In fact that's probably why we're having this conversation—you know, it comes out one way or another. Marvin listens resolutely, a fixed smile on his face. His cane is beside him, his neck sticks out of his collar like a dried carrot, but he wears a red flannel jacket and plaid vest, cheerful as Christmas. The awareness comes over us, a collective decision, and everyone begins to talk privately to his dinner partner.

This is the latest thing, people with cancer going out for the evening. What an appalling trend, *not being afraid*! Is Death just another evening out?

Climbing up the subway steps at Astor Place I came upon a sidewalk market: bootleg tapes, clothes with the labels cut, handbags, wallets, newly published books spread on plastic sheets on the pavement. Smiling young men in watch caps and torn fatigue jackets stood behind these values. I saw them just last year in Lima. I saw them afterward in Mexico City. The wave is lapping at our shore. There are many Iranians now living in Los Angeles. Vietnamese distributed along the West Coast. Laotian men suffering sudden-death syndrome in their tract homes in the Rockies, Haitians wading ashore in Florida, Salvadorans, Guatemalans, streaming over the river into Texas. Dear God, let them migrate, let my country be the last best hope. But let us make some distinctions here: The Irish, the Italians, the Jews of Eastern Europe, came here because they wanted a new life. They worked for the money to bring over their families. They said good riddance to the old country and were glad to be gone. They did not come here because of something we had done to them. The new immigrants are here because we have made their lands unlivable. They have come here to save themselves from us. They have brought their hot politics with them. They have set up their paramilitary camps. They're murdering each other. The secret police of their own countries are flying here to murder them. Bombs from the *repúblicas* explode on Connecticut Avenue. My President embraces sociopaths wearing medals of murder on their chests. Beggars scrounge in the garbage. The eyes of the barrio stare at me. In October last year, going to a Halloween party in Mexico City at the residence of an American cultural attaché, a house protected like all of them by iron gates, I pushed through a cluster of mestizos, leather-skin people of indeterminate age, some carrying infants in colored bindings slung from their shoulders, and they were holding out their fedoras, saying something in their soft toothless diction, and I figured it out, trick or treat, trick or treat, a murmur, no anger in it, trick or treat, like the sound of a gentle flock of ground birds.

It is possible something really serious has happened to me. It is possible I've become estranged from my calling. But how can that

be? I have followed it in fidelity, step by step, I have tracked it in
its logic, I have never wavered, I have been steadfast, and it has led
me to this desert, this flat horizon. I turn around and around and
I'm alone. Is there a specific doom that comes of commitment?
You cross some invisible limit, in logic and in faith, and a nameless
universe blows through your eyes. It is possible I have crossed. I
once wanted to write a novel about Bishop Pike. I see now why, I
see the connection, I must have recognized the eye-rolling worship, the white-knuckled faith that takes you right through it, that
punches through the magma. The good bishop, still wearing his
collar, followed his love of God where it took him, into the occul-
tist camp. His son had died of an overdose and there was this me-
dium who could put him in touch with his dead son. Oh what
grief, what grief. The Book of Common Prayer falls from the
fingers. If you truly believe in God, how can you not crave the
supernatural? If He can be prayed to why can't He come off a
Ouija board, in a darkened parlor, on the choked voice of a con
man? The bishop never thought he'd left the see, poor mad fuck,
disappearing into the Negev with a bottle of Coke.

Once, years ago, my friend Arlington came to our house in Connecticut and stayed over. We heard him moaning in his sleep. But
in the morning I found him sitting with my children at the breakfast
table. Big man, built like a nose tackle, sitting there in his ribbed
undershirt, a Pall Mall in one hand, a full tumbler of bourbon in the
other. Arlington had a photographic memory and his idea of conversation was to recite poems. He'd ad-lib whole anthologies of things
he's read and loved. So there were my kids, quite small at the time,
sitting in front of their Rice Krispies, spoons in their fists, and they
were staring at him and forgetting to eat. And there was Angel in
her bathrobe at the kitchen counter making peanut-butter sand-
wiches for the lunch bags and shaking her head in disbelief. And

there was I clutching my coffee cup and trying to bring my eyes to focus. And James Arlington coming off *Green Groweth the Holly*, dragged on his cigarette, pulled on his bourbon, and went into a poem of Trakl's about German fascist decadence. And it wasn't yet eight o'clock in the morning.

Ah this poet, just to show you what a memory he had: We were classmates at Kenyon. There were lots of poets on campus, poetry was what we did at Kenyon, the way at Ohio State they played football. And three or four of the collegiate poets were good and promising, like Arlington, but there were bad poets too, and poetasters, and precious aesthetes, and we liked to make fun of them, the rarefied sensibility of them. One autumn day, walking with Jim, I jumped into a pile of leaves and threw and kicked them into the air, and as they fell around my head, fluttering and spinning, I held up one limp wrist and lifted my chin and cried out in trembling appreciation, The leaves are falling, the leaves are falling! Arlington loved that, he laughed his loud brassy helpless laugh, this true poet who loved to listen to records of Elisabeth Schwarzkopf singing lieder but also liked to sing "Sam Sam the Shithouse Man" as he walked down the middle path—this central Ohio farmhand among the fraternity boys in their gray flannels and white bucks. And for weeks afterward he would regale me, The leaves are falling, look look, the leaves are falling! It became part of his repertoire of total recall, he remembered our lines for us all—we were the misfits, the outcasts, the pariahs of that campus, and he gathered us around him and gave us our pride, our edge—he remembered for us the lines and routines by which we sought his appreciation. All right, and thirty years go by, and he is a famous poet, he lives with the helpless intensity, and raging submission to poetry, of the doomed. And he is a prodigious drinker, a monstrous drinker, and finally, age fifty, he decides to dry out, and that becomes the struggle, the torment, staying sober. And he's working on it and keeping away from it, looking thinner now, that derelict pallor they get, and in this state comes down with the sore throat that turns out to be cancer. And I visit him one day in the hospital and by now he can't speak, they've packed his mouth with some sort of medicated batting, and he has a grommet sewn in the neck to keep open a tracheotomy so he can breathe, and he motions to his wife, Molly, for the clipboard and he writes on it and hands it to me and in the same farmboy scrawl of thirty years ago it says: The Leaves Are Falling.

Of course she lives in the Berkshires. I say of course. As a child I spent summers there and it hasn't changed. It is a home of the spirit for me. All it took was one walk in the hushed umber wood. My footfall on the pine-needle floor. The hovering dragonfly turning slowly in a column of clear light. I came upon a gorge with its waterspill striking sound from the white boulders. Melville lived there, and Hawthorne, who taught me Romance, and even William Cullen Bryant. And she lives there. Once, in winter, we went to an inn thirty miles from her town. Though she is single she's the more discreet of us, she's suffered gossip, she paid for her Ph.D. by teaching grade school, but whatever she's accomplished there has always been someone to say her looks are what did it, she is sensitive about this. So we had best not be seen together. All right with me. She wore a dark fitted coat and under it a lovely high-waisted white dress with blue fleurs-de-lis. We had a drink in the bar and went to our room. There was a chenille spread on the four-poster. I pulled the shades behind the white curtains. There were two of those small upholstered wing chairs you can't really sit in. A clawfoot tub in the bath. We took off our clothes and made love.

No matter how you've thought about what it would be like, what rage of tumescence you bring to it, when she removes her clothes it becomes very humanly specific, a body with an odd line here, a roundness there, a thickness in the thighs or a touching narrowness of the shoulders, breasts not as large as she would like, or some misproportion, long hair too full and long for the body, there is some triumph or tyranny of ordinary life, a female protest against ideal form, and you, of course, in your own specific fate, take her in your arms and all your lust turns pure and curiously calm and you laugh to find yourself simply and innocently making love with another person.

Late at night the hour came to take her home. We drove the thirty miles to her town. It was late and very cold. The road curved between banks of snow, dark woods rose on the hills on either side of us. She pointed out the few stars that could be seen on this black night. I turned off the headlights. She laughed in terror. I coasted without lights down the curving hills. With both her hands she held on to my arm, her fingers squeezed my arm and she laughed and shivered as we hurtled along, a dark shape in the dark road under the stars.

She always scrupulously refused presents except if they were of the smallest value. And she gave me things all the time—flowers, ornamental spoons, antique postcards, a bud vase, little offerings of moments of her thought, always beautiful and well chosen.

I left her at the edge of her hill town where she had parked her car. The river was ice. A wind blew up snow along the streets. At river's edge, a boarded-up mill of red brick.

Yet here is her pretty card of foreign mountains, distant passes. The Himalayas. *I have met some people and am going on with them. Forgive me.* She has met some people and is going on with them. She has turned herself into a pretty postcard of foreign mountains, distant skies. I trace her ink with my finger. Once she said to me: Language is something that almost isn't there.

In the sciences too, not just religion: Linus Pauling with the Nobel in Chemistry going on to make these claims for the curative powers of vitamin C in megadoses, going on in logic, in faith, till they take his research money away, fault his data. Pauling, a genial man in his seventies, absolutely imperturbable, reeling off the discouragements matter-of-factly, without complaint, telling what he knows to black-tie dinners. Science is now some walled city he's been put out of, he stands there at the gates with the other peddlers, he has followed his calling where it took him.

And of course the classic case of Wilhelm Reich. There was a moment there when Freud thought he was the best of them. Made great contributions to the psychoanalytic literature. Went marching on, in logic, and in faith, to the idea of curing all of society. Went marching, in his doom of commitment, smack into the orgone box. Walked out of it somewhere in New Hampshire to end his life shooting down UFO's with a tin ray gun of his own design.

A call from my mother: I saw your friend Norman's name in the newspaper, I see him all the time on television, why don't I ever see you on television? I don't know, Mom, I value my privacy. Why, she says, what are you hiding?

He says a lot of them are sick from malnutrition, they eat only tortillas and beans so he teaches them about nourishment in the leaves of yucca trees, or papaya. He says a great medical aid is the common nail, which, when left in their water for a few days, supplies them with the iron they need to cure their anemia. He says there is no aspirin so he teaches them to make tea from willow-tree bark, which is an analgesic. A brew of eucalyptus leaves is a cough suppressant. He says if the National Guard catches someone with medical supplies, a few bars of soap, some vials of tetanus antitoxin, they take him in as a subversive.

I am trying to remember everything he said. We listened in a loft on Spring Street, grown men and women sitting on the floor like children while this pale young doctor stood by the pillars and spoke. It's not jungle where you can hide. It's farmland, hills and valleys, and every bit of it is lived on, so the guerrillas have to depend on the people. Each zone of control is run by general assembly elected from the community. Each zone plants its own crops, but they warehouse the harvests collectively. Some of the zones specialize in poultry breeding or raising pigs or goats. They have just a few primitive hospitals. They train paramedicals called *brigadistas* to help the few doctors and med students. They hold reading and writing classes under the trees.

I am sitting and listening to the young doctor. I have chosen to put my back to the wall. My knees are drawn up. I open my eyes and see out the big dusty loft window to my own building a few blocks to the north. I count up nine stories and see my own lights. I think of myself standing in the window looking back at me. It comes to me why I took this apartment. I took it for her. I took it for our New York place.

When the government attacks a particular zone the guerrillas evacuate the civilians at the same time they fight back. They carry the wounded with them. They hide the livestock. They leave at night. It's all very well organized, he says. When the incursion is over the civilians are brought back. Most of the guerrillas are under eighteen. They hold reading and writing classes under the trees.

She has met some people? What people! Who are these friends of hers! How does she get to all these countries, no visible means of support?

CIA cunt.

Who's around, someone's got to pay. The heart, breaking, gives the taste of blood. Who's around? You were supposed to be a girl, my mother said to me when I was five, I wanted a daughter for my old age. He gave me *some time,* she told her friends one day on some mountain porch at dusk, nineteen-thirty-what?—I playing on the wooden steps, my eyes level with the monumental feminine calves and knees, thighs spread on the wicker chairs, skirts pulled back to find the breeze of this hot mountain twilight *a breech birth, I thought he'd kill me.* Rilke had it worse, who had everything worse, his mother named him Renee and dressed him in girl's clothes and wouldn't cut his hair. Rainer is what he changed it to when he grew up. Rainer Maria Rilke. Why didn't he do something about the Maria while he was at it? *Here there is no place that does not see you. You must change your life.* Yes, Renee/Rainer. Seek transfiguration. Deliver the wet shining soul. For Death will make a story of you. It will say you have done the right thing. That you've added to the stock of blessed beings and made a modest run. Oh Love, I don't like the word on me, this drift through the blood of my obsolescence. That my biological time is over. That I've used up the world. That I'm no longer incredibly good-looking.

Theodora S. is around, I met her at the Grand Union the other day. She told me her husband had left her for another woman: And for his sake I gave up a meaningful affair, she said. No, not Theodora.

The tall Icelander? Last time we talked she had found a wonderful new diet and taken off several pounds. She said she was looking for an exercise to keep them off. Why not sex, I suggested. You burn two hundred calories each time out. Surely not if you just lie there, she said. No, not the tall Icelander.

And as his brain was just lying there, his bloodshot open eye understood it was perceiving, restless on the floor, while the saintly doctor spoke, so restless she couldn't get her legs under herself comfortably, skirt riding up, lot of leg showing, good God, his, my, old actress friend Brenda. Brenda was for five minutes some years ago my hot muse. We hit it off because she knew so much more than I about illness and disease. Not just vivacious and sexy, who isn't these days, but a great authority on physical misfortune. There she is. We are staring across the room smiling at each other, hearing of them holding reading and writing classes under the trees.

Brenda miraculously pulled through brain surgery a few years ago and told me when we met she could expect a severe palsy in old age as a kind of delayed aftereffect. If she lived that long. She still took Atabrine for the malaria she'd picked up in Bangladesh and when I knew her she suffered from pelvic inflammatory disease although I thought it was me doing that to her, I thought it was me. Fine, spooky actress, and a good kisser, too. With that poetic gift they have in the theater to feel harder and more desperately than anyone else. We'll go away somewhere and live poor, she said in the flush of our friendship, I can make you so happy! Her leg is scarred from a time a crazy Vietnam vet beat her up at a rally, kicked her and broke the tibia, which the doctor then didn't set properly. Or was it a car accident, I don't remember. She'd broken a lot of bones and I could see how. One night, at a benefit reading a bunch of us gave in Southampton, she was afterward assailed by some fans, and to get away she did this astonishing thing, backed up to the porch railing and true, it was not more than eight or ten steps off the ground, but she back-flipped right over the rail and disappeared in a flounce of petticoats, strap shoes kicking, we all stood there looking at each other too stunned to do anything, listening to Brenda thrashing about in the privet hedge.

I became wary when I began to add up all the stories she told me of directors who'd beat on her, stars who'd tried to rape her, deathly illnesses she'd survived, political intrigues in which she had put her life in danger. It would have been all right if she were some kind of mythomaniac, but she was telling the absolute truth. Unthinkable. You don't get a cold in that league, you get pneumonia. You go on a vacation somewhere and a revolution breaks out. You're a lightning rod for life, you turn white-hot, you burn up. I want to live a long time, I don't *want* to live poor, I don't want seven different but simultaneous diseases fighting over me.

But here we were talking again after the American Doctor-Saint's talk in the Spring Street loft of the faithful and I was remembering how good and warm she was to hold, tall long-waisted woman, she once actually got me to dance, why I even promised to write a play for her, and here she is again talking, laughing, her eyes going wide with wonder, like a child's, and I am thinking heaven sent, heaven sent, with several drinks in me I may begin to hope I have not been devastated. I may hope I am a comedian and my fate is of no consequence.

So checks are written for their medical supplies and I shake hands with the speaker and Brenda and I go along to a café and we talk, and then to a bar on Prince Street, and we talk some more, she tells me what she's doing these days, what she's into. Oh Jonathan, she says, I'm so afraid of going back down there. But how can I not? Oh God, you know what they do to rebel women? She shivers and drinks. We sit close, I put my arm around her, warm sweet thing. We drink. Oh Jonathan, there's so much to do, she says. She's in New York for just a couple of days, she's staying with a friend. I tell her no need for that, she can spend the night with me. Perhaps I should have paid attention. She looks into my eyes. She takes my hand and by and by, don't ask me how, we are in a church vestry on the Upper West Side and I am shaking hands with a red-bearded rector in a clerical collar, and he says in the way they use that verb he wants to share something with me, and, indeed generously, he lays his weird cabalistic lore on me, he tells me how many of them are living illegally in the various church sanctuary programs, or passing through to Canada like the old underground railroad, and it is quite a few, we look in his office, we look in the church library, we look in the basement meeting room, and everywhere in the nightlit shadows are rows of beds and the dark shapes of people sleeping like my days in summer camp on those little iron cots. We return to light and I see Brenda hanging on his arm and looking at his mouth as he speaks, gazing in his clear handsome young countenance.

Sometime in the last five years things became serious. I hadn't noticed. No wonder they're all getting the better of me.

What will I do with these postcards of love, this ornamental spoon, this vase, this cut-glass bowl? Her womby vessels. See if I can drop them cleanly nine stories down the incinerator without touching the sides.

Feeling this wretched, I decided after all to go last night to Crenshaw's publication party at the Dakota. I wanted to take comfort and remember what it is we do. My esteemed colleague has somehow worked it out that by writing a weak but circumlocutious novel every three or four years and having parties thrown for him at famous salons, he maintains a legendary literary status. It's a wonderful thing, he expects to be honored, and so he is. Every writer who's in town is there, Norman and Kurt, Joyce, Angel has driven down from Connecticut with Bill and Rose—Angel looking terrific, where'd she get that dress? Jonathan, she says, laughing, how nice to see you—I wave to Phil, there's Bernie, John, John A., Peter and Maria in from the Island . . . We are all here save for a few of Crenshaw's enemies and we're all deferring in our own separate manners, not the least me, to this effigy of ourselves, the Great Success, whom we would worship and send up in flames simultaneously.

Starry night! Difficult to talk, we're being mobbed out. I'm introduced to a young woman. How do you do, I say. I thought you were cleverer than that, she says. The apartment a dozen or so rooms of high ceilings, a Balthus here, a de Kooning Woman there, elegant antique rugs, the backing worn through, lots of polished floor and bare window. The place is jammed, flashbulbs pop, a crowd around

Boy George, what's he/she doing here? This season the fellows wearing their hair short, with arrow-sharp sideburns. Black suits over white undershirts. The girls with Detroit cuts, or porcupines, big red lips, long box coats and ankle warmers.

I start drinking. My dear colleague Leo holds the high ground just to the side and slightly to the rear of a bar table so he can get his refills without standing in the three-deep mob in front. He is a deeply serious drinker and the bartender understands this and respects it. Leo's a large unkempt being, tie loose, shirt half pulled out of his pants, uncombed hair fallen in a shock over one eye, he sweats so, he looks as if he's in meltdown, he's always looked this way. Writing for Leo is absolute and irremediable torture, a chronic degenerative disease, a book comes from him not more than once in ten years, he's quite brilliant and has never made a dime, and he's of an age when the grants and fellowships are yokes around his neck. Tell me, he says, looking me in the eye, is there a writer here who really believes in what he's doing? Does any one of us have a true conviction for what he's writing? Do I? Do you?

Just what I needed. Tearful eyes of umbrage await my answer. Oh Leo, I think, when you make a little money from your work you'll see what trouble is. His wife, glamorous in a kind of draped dress, plucks from his tie a crumb of taco chip. He looks at her hand and watches it rise past his nose: she combs the shock of hair back from his forehead. Woman, you trouble me, he says, and walks into the crowd.

Oh Leo, I wanted to say, each book has taken me further and further out so that the occasion itself is extenuated, no more than a weak distant signal from the home station, and even that may be fading.

A call from Ron, my lawyer. He puts one of his partners on the conference line who's a specialist in immigration and naturalization cases. It is a definitely illegal act. The federal law provides for a fine as high as two thousand dollars and/or a jail sentence to a maximum of five years. You sure they're undocumented? Ron asks. There are a lot of them here legally who are just down and out. No, no, the real thing, I tell him. It may be just for a few days. Till they find a safe place for them. I feel heroic. Daring. Well, the partner says, to date the INS has done nothing about these programs. They haven't raided the churches or anything like that. But as this thing grows they'll have to come down on it, try a test case or two, make an example. In any event we have to advise you not to engage in activities that are criminal under the law.

I call the church. The good father of the clear countenance says I thought we were together in this. Christ, give these people an inch. Well, look, I say, I want to help out but I have to confess I had in mind a less fervent participation, something along the lines of a modest good deed. What do you want me to do, the father who is younger than I am says, we're up against it, we're overextended, their beds are already taken. This is what it means to bear witness.

Hands me that theological shit.

How do I feel? I don't care anymore. Maybe like that poet in Yeats who lies down to die on the king's doorstep because he's been kicked out of the ruling circle. Yeah, that's what this place is, that's what I'm doing here, and if I die, let the curse be on their heads. What else can this mean except I've been deprived of my ancient right to matter? Yes, you mothers, I of the Untitled Thread Mills, a mere man of words, will sit once more in the councils of state or a dire desolation will erupt from the sky, drift like a fire-filled fog over the World Trade Center, glut the streets of SoHo with its sulfurous effulgence, shriek through every cracked window, stop the singing voice of every living soul, and make of your diversified investment portfolio a useless thing.

A call to Angel. She has trouble understanding. Another tricky surprise, something *else* I'm doing to her? She makes me doubt myself. Don't ask me these questions, I say. I, least of anyone, know what I'm capable of. Think about yourself, I tell her in the frau doctor's head lingo, we're separate people, you decide for yourself what you want to do. You can sleep on it. No, Jonathan, she says, I'm trying to tell you I'm pleased to be asked.

And so, *mis amigos,* there he was early one morning on the IRT. The way we travel now. Graffiti car empty except for the family sitting across from him, Father Mother Three Kids staring at me eyes big and dark as plums, fold-up stroller several suitcases wrapped in clothesline to keep from springing open, one squirming infant on the lap. He can't breathe too well, little snot bubble forms and breaks on each and every exhalation. They are neat, trim people, dressed in clean church donations. The ad overhead. I am reading, practicing my Spanish, I see now why: *El estar sentado todo el día es malo para mis hemorroides. Quiero una medicina que ayude a reducir la hinchazón.* Oh yes I'll need a lot of that, a whole case for the case I've got now.

And this morning I'm writing, here it is a new day of the late winter, the Mrs. is cooking up some gruel in the kitchen, they have brought their own tortilla mix and dried beans, the kids are well behaved but beginning to explore the apartment, something just broke in the bathroom, there is an exhortation, a head pokes in, apologias, baby diapers are not the best-smelling things in the world, it serves me right, wait'll the boys hear about this, I have to get lots of things in here that I never needed before, pots pans, more dishes, soap for the basement clothes washer, quarters, I have to make sure they remember we come in and out through the basement. My friend the Señor is miserable, awfully thin, high cheekbones, black mustache, that black straight mestizo hair they have, he stands at the picture window in the finest digs he's ever seen in his life and stares at the skyline thinking what has happened to my life.

What has happened to *my* life!

I'll need sheets for cots, I'll need cots, I haven't got that much time today, I'm waiting for Angel in the 245DL, does this mean I'll have to live in Connecticut? Let's not get carried away. Maybe they'll really only stay a day or two, maybe they'll get arrested. Look, my country, what you've done to me, what I have to do to live with myself.

And on the news on the radio they think they've discovered a new planet system orbiting around the star Vega, they're not sure yet, a big dust cloud, an infant system, the first ever seen going around anything besides our sun, yes, and just in time too, it'll be close in any event.

Little kid here wants to type. OK, I hold his finger, we're typing now, I lightly press his tiny index finger, the key, striking, delights him, each letter suddenly struck vvv he likes the v, hey who's writing this? every good boy needs a toy boat, maybe we'll go to the bottom of the page get my daily quota done come on, kid, you can do three more lousy lines

E. L. Doctorow was born in New York City and
educated at Kenyon College and Columbia Univer-
sity. He is the author of five novels, *Welcome to
Hard Times, Big as Life, The Book of Daniel,
Ragtime* and *Loon Lake,* and a play,
Drinks Before Dinner.